Open Wounds, Secret Obsessions

STORIES

Linda Joyce Ott

Published by GUNLIN, 144 Holton Ave. S., Hamilton
Ontario Canada L8M 2L5

For Günter

Contents

Keeper of the Gown

I remember the day she came in. It was Monday after lunch. We had just finished the "sort" and were outside enjoying tea and smokes.

The beginning of the week was always full of surprises because we needed to sort through the bags of cast-offs that people had dropped in front of the doors on Sunday. We are closed Sundays and our weekday hours are clearly posted, but still every Monday morning a heap of plastic bags and cardboard boxes full of old clothes and household stuff would greet us.

Some people certainly thought of this place as the local dump, so a lot of the stuff in the "sort" went straight into the rag pile, or the garbage. We had to be careful though, because sometimes treasures were mixed in with the junk.

One time Enid found an alligator purse in a garbage bag filled with worn blankets and sheets. The same day I found a pair of black leather gloves with the price tag still on. I would have missed them if I hadn't shaken out every one of the musty-smelling sweaters carefully folded in a liquor store box.

It was a typical June day — sunny, hot, and humid according to the weather network — muggy, sweaty and unbearable according to those of us who worked without air conditioning. She was gazing at the window display. It was one of our best. We had dressed the mannequins in sleeveless floral shifts and bathing suits, then added paperbacks for dog-day reading, plastic glasses on trays, lawn chairs and a wading pool.

She was about my height, in her early twenties I would guess, and looked as cool as a popsicle, in a powder blue silk suit with matching purse and shoes. She hesitated in the doorway and then walked purposefully up to the counter. No one was there. Martha had finished her cigarette and dashed off to the drug store across the street to get some tampons. Enid had just gone to the ladies' room.

I stubbed out my second cigarette, gulped down the rest of my tea, and went in.

"Can I help you?" I asked.

"Yes, I think so," she said in a voice so quiet I could hardly hear her. "You see, I have this."

She laid a big white box, embossed in gold with the words *Dream Shoppe*, on the counter. She undid the shiny pink ribbon around the box and opened it to reveal the most beautiful dress I'd ever seen, a snow white, satin and lace wedding gown.

"Oh my," I said.

It was the dress of every girl's dreams. Silver filigree

embroidered roses covered the bodice. Tiny rosebud-shaped glass buttons started at the waist and went up to the exquisitely formed scoop neckline.

She lifted it gently out of the box, removing sheet after sheet of delicately scented tissue paper. For a moment she smiled as she held the gown in front of her. The satin skirt billowed out into a five-foot long lace train. Then brusquely, she thrust the gown back into its box.

"Brand new, never worn," she said. "The veil's here too. I was wondering if you'd take it. For the store, I mean, to sell."

"Of course," I said, "but we can't pay you for it. We only accept donations."

"That's okay. I didn't pay for it either," she said. "I just hope someone gets more happiness out of it than I did."

Before I could thank her, she was gone.

I gazed at the gown in the box. If only, I thought. Then just as quickly banished the idea from my mind. Even if Mike asked me, he'd never agree to a church wedding. I'd be lucky to get him to City Hall.

Martha and Enid returned and found me in a daze. I showed them the gown and told them about the woman in blue. We decided to change the window display right away. Usually we wait until Thursday, but a garment such as this deserved special treatment.

We ransacked the store looking for accessories that would do justice to the gown. By quitting time, we had all the elements together: white pumps, a sequined evening bag, a peach-coloured gown for the mother of the bride, a floral dress for the flower girl, a couple of wine glasses, a lace tablecloth and a slightly tarnished silver candelabra.

Like little girls playing with a dollhouse, we spent all the next morning arranging our bridal window. By noon it was done. It looked absolutely fabulous.

Before it was finished, each of us had taken turns trying on the dream dress and posing like mannequins in the window display. We took pictures of each other with my cell phone so we wouldn't forget how beautiful we looked.

Martha couldn't do up the zipper once she got the gown on, but that didn't show up in the picture. With her tousled golden hair, flushed cheeks and joyous smile, she looked like Glinda, the good witch in *The Wizard of Oz*.

The dress was too long for Enid but we just spread it around her and didn't let her walk in it. In the photo, she looked as fragile as a porcelain figurine.

Me? It fitted perfectly. All that afternoon, I couldn't take my eyes off the pictures of me in the gown. It was unreal. I looked like Princess Di. If only I could broach the subject with Mike. Maybe just showing him the pictures would change his mind.

The first week that it stood in the window, the gown was never far from our thoughts or conversation. We wondered about the woman who had brought it in. Was she stood up at the altar, or did her fiancé die in an accident? And we had to decide what to charge for it.

Enid said we probably shouldn't sell it because it would bring bad luck, having been bought and not used.

"At least we need to warn people about it," she said,

twisting her wedding band on and off.

"That's ridiculous," I said. "Next thing you'll believe is that that it's unlucky if my black cat walks in front of you."

Martha, who couldn't even fit in the gown, felt that we'd have to be careful who we sold it to.

"If we charge too much, somebody who really needs it might not be able to afford it," she said. "Besides we got it for free, so couldn't we just give it to someone needy?"

Enid felt we should take the names of people who wanted it and have a draw.

"Like the lottery," she said, "we'll sell tickets for five dollars and then pick a winner."

But nobody was interested in the gown. A lot of people stopped and stared at the window display, yet all that first week, not one person came in to ask about it.

The next Monday I saw the woman who had brought in the gown. I had just finished having a smoke when I glanced across the street. She was standing in the shade wearing sun glasses and looking at our display. I don't know how long she'd been there. When I waved, she hurried away.

We left the display up for a month. We sold both the mother of the bride's dress and the flower girl's but no one asked about the gown.

Then the day before we were going to take it down, a young girl and her mother came into the store. After lots of loud talk, in what I think was Portuguese, accompanied by a great deal of hand waving, the girl shyly asked if she could try on the gown.

"My mother wants to know how much it is?" she said as

she carried it into the tiny cubicle that served as our change room.

I hesitated. Then glancing at her mother all dressed in black, her arms folded tightly across her massive bosom, I said, "It's brand new, never been worn. Seventy-five dollars cash, no cheques, no layaways."

The girl tried on the gown. It fit as if it were made for her.

I called Enid and Martha over. The girl smiled and posed in front of the mirror until her mother said something. When she came out of the change room clutching the gown in her arms, her mother snapped open her purse and counted out the bills.

"It looks like it was made for you," I said as I folded the gown back into its tissue wrappings and laid it tenderly in the box. "When's the wedding?"

"Next month," she said and pointed to her tummy. "It has to be soon, before it shows. I didn't want a white gown but my mother will disown me if I don't have a proper church wedding."

Getting pregnant, that was one way to tie the knot. I had shown Mike the pictures of me in the gown. He was unimpressed.

"It's a little early for Hallowe'en," he had said.

I said that we were only trying to liven up the window display and never mentioned the gown to him again.

There was a full moon out and my period was due any day which may be why I snapped at Enid later that evening when she bummed another cigarette off of me.

"Christ Enid, if you've quit, you've quit. Make up your mind and stick to it."

When Martha poked me to point out this gorgeous hunk who came in to look through the tennis rackets, I reminded her that I already had a boyfriend.

"And he's a bit young for you," I said.

We took the rest of the display down the next day and put up one with a picnic in the park theme.

"It doesn't do much for me," I said as we stood across the street and studied it. "I guess I'm kind of tired of summer stuff."

About a week later, the woman who had brought in the wedding gown was back. She wanted to talk to me, although either Enid or Martha could have answered her questions just as well.

"You probably don't remember me," she said. "I brought in a wedding gown. You had it in your window for a while. I was just wondering what had happened to it?"

I told her about the girl and her mother.

"Was she pretty?"

I nodded.

"But pregnant, you say? And still going to wear a white gown? What a shame. I'm rather surprised you let her buy it."

Several weeks later, I was alone at the front counter reading Danielle Steel's latest bestseller when the young girl's mother walked in carrying the *Dream Shoppe* box.

"Excuse me," she said as she hefted the box onto the counter. "I want money back. Seventy-five dollars. I give you back this."

"Sorry," I said and pointed to the sign behind me. "No exchanges or refunds. That's our policy."

She shook her head and began to untie the box. I got goose-bumps when I saw the gown again. It lay in the box exactly as I had folded it several weeks earlier.

"No good," she said. "You give me back seventy-five dollars. Here is gown."

I knew I should ask Ted, the manager, but he wouldn't be in until tomorrow. I checked the till. Seventy-five dollars would just about clean us out. I hesitated then looked at the gown once more.

"Was the wedding cancelled?"

She took a handkerchief from her sleeve and dabbed her eyes.

"No wedding. Baby die."

I gave her the money. She stuffed it in her handbag and left.

The door hadn't closed behind her before I unwrapped the gown and laid it over the counter. It still took my breath away. We decided not to put it in the window but hung it instead next to the party dresses.

That Saturday night I was the last one in the store at closing time. Mike was away all weekend on a fishing trip with the guys, so I took the gown home.

It was a dumb thing to do. I spilled red wine on it and had a heck of a time washing it out. As I danced around the apartment, the cat thought I was playing and got his claws caught in the satin hem. But I really don't think anyone would notice the few tiny holes he made.

On Monday morning I got in to work before the others and hung the gown back up with the party dresses.

The next week a plain-faced woman in her thirties tried it on. It was a bit large for her. She fussed and frowned a lot looking at herself in the mirror, so I thought she wouldn't want it.

"It's not exactly right," she said to Martha. "What do you think? It has to be perfect. I wouldn't want it if it wasn't. It has to be perfect."

Martha tried to reassure her.

"It's never been worn, you know. It's a real bargain, custom-made."

The woman stood on tip-toes and did pirouettes twirling the gown giddily around her. Then she began giggling.

"I just don't know, I just don't know," she said over and over.

"Something old, something new, something borrowed, something blue," she chanted.

I was about to interfere, but Martha was irritated as well.

"Please take it off. Either buy it or leave it. We don't want it ruined, you know. It's not a costume."

The woman pouted but took off the gown.

"I'll take it," she said. "It's got to be perfect. The wedding's going to be so big. Everyone will be there. There'll be dancing, and lots of food and buckets of champagne. Ou là là! Flowers everywhere. It's in a garden. You must come. It'll be perfect."

I got the box out. Martha wrapped the gown up. Only

after it was boxed, did we discover that she didn't have seventy-five dollars.

Martha looked at me. I nodded. We took the forty-three dollars she had and escorted her out the door with wishes of luck and promises to attend the wedding.

Early the next day, a heavy-set woman appeared at the door before opening time. She held a large box. It was bashed in and dirty but I recognized it immediately. I unlocked the door.

"Sorry to trouble you my dear, but I've got a bit of a problem," she said. "One of our patients apparently bought this gown here yesterday. Well, it's not quite the right thing for her. She puts it on and then sits in a corner crying.

"I know you don't usually take things back, but we're dealing with someone who's quite ill. Really she shouldn't have spent all her money. She has no spending money for the next month unless you take this back."

Ted hadn't been too thrilled when he learned about the seventy-five dollars when the gown was first returned. But now he couldn't say much, because we were dealing with a mental case.

After the woman left, I took the gown out of the box. Grass stains were smeared over the train. One of the rosebud buttons hung loosely from a thread. The veil was torn. Tearfully, I showed the gown to Martha. I told her that I would take it home to mend and clean.

I kept the gown at home for nearly a month. Mike and I had broken up so it was okay to keep it there. I sewed and cleaned it, and almost every night after work, I'd wear it, sip some wine and imagine what my life would be like – if only.

One day though, I overheard Martha and Enid talking about me. They spoke about the wedding gown as though I'd stolen it. I didn't let on that I'd heard them, but the next day I brought it in.

"Good as new," I said. "It was harder than I thought to get those grass stains out. Shall we put it in the window?"

It was close to Hallowe'en when we sold the gown again. A waif-like girl with burgundy ponytails and her bald-headed boyfriend had come in to search out costumes.

As soon as the girl saw the wedding gown, she screeched, "Charlie, look here. Picture it. I'll dye my hair black and get black lipstick and fingernails. It'll be to die for."

I sold the gown to Charlie for twenty dollars and never expected to see it again. But the day after Hallowe'en, our local newspaper featured the girl in the wedding gown as the *Bride of Frankenstein* with other costumed ghoulies and ghastlies on the front page. Seven people had been seriously injured in a brawl in the after hours club where a Hallowe'en party had taken place.

The next Monday, I discovered the gown in the "sort". I nearly cried when I saw it. Black stains were smeared across the bodice. Red marks that looked like blood were streaked all over the gown. The bottom was cut in zig-zags and a long thigh-high slit ran up one side.

I threw it in the rag pile, but I couldn't get it out of my mind.

Before the pile was picked up that afternoon, I grabbed the gown, put it in a garbage bag and stashed it under the front counter.

At home I washed it by hand and mended the rips and fraying hem as best I could. On many evenings when I have nothing better to do, I put it on and sit in my rocker, eating chocolate and sipping wine, being ever so careful not to spill any on my wedding gown.

Mother Mourning

I'm staring out the window of the bus, stroking my swollen tummy when I see her. She's pushing a shopping cart crammed with rags and bags. I see a boot, a broken umbrella and several torn blankets squashed between layers of bulging grocery store bags. She shuffles along, stopping every few feet to yell at the passing traffic. Her long matted grey hair frames a weather-beaten face. As the bus stops beside her, my eyes catch, and for an instant, hold hers. Through the dirty window, I am transfixed by the realization that those piercing pale blue eyes, red-rimmed and crusted, belong to my mother.

The bus lurches forward. I pull the cord to get off. By the time I return to where I saw her, she has disappeared. I scan the park, then circle the block, checking out alleys, and calling "mummy" over and over, as if she were a lost cat.

In a Tim Horton's, I sit by the window, gulping a glass of cold milk and gobbling two chocolate donuts. I remember it clearly. Peter and I are crying. Mummy gets up abruptly, slips on a sweater, grabs her purse and leaves. There are no good-byes.

Or was it the fight? Daddy's drunk again. He slaps her across the face and tells her she can get the fuck out of his life. Later, when he's passed out and Peter and I are asleep, she packs her suitcase, kisses us and leaves.

Or she's having an affair with the milkman. They plot their escape. When he comes to deliver the milk, she leaves with the empties.

Anyway you look at it, it's an unsolved mystery. One day she's there; the next gone. No good-byes, no fight, no note, nothing.

When the cramps hit, I clutch the tabletop and continue to scrutinize each passerby. All at once I feel a warm leaking between my thighs and hurry outside to flag down a taxi. The cabby eyes me warily when I tell him I want to go to St. Jo's.

"Don't worry," I say, heaving my bulk into the back seat, "it's only for a check-up."

My due date had passed but at my appointment yesterday, Dr. Stern said that first babies were often late.

This morning, in a burst of energy, I went to the mall. In Sears' baby department, I picked up and put down dozens of tiny items in as many minutes.

"Just looking," I mumbled to the clerk who hovered, cooing as I fondled bootie after bootie.

Buying nothing, I headed to cosmetics. There the sleek sales ladies busied themselves at my approach. Left alone, I massaged aromatic lotions onto my hands and soaked my wrists and neck with heady perfumes.

The taxi seems to hit every red light. Each time the driver brakes, I jerk forward, closing my eyes and stifling a moan. A few blocks from the hospital, I gasp loudly.

"I'm going as fast as I can," the driver yells, nodding toward the lanes of traffic snarled alongside. "Is this your first?"

By the time we get to St. Jo's, I've told the driver more about myself than anyone knows. I burst into tears when he refuses the twenty dollars I hand him.

"Keep it," he says, "the first gift for your newborn." He runs around the cab to open the door. "Thank you for not having the baby in my car. I just this month paid it off."

I stuff the money in my purse and shuffle into the hospital, pausing at each cramp. As I wait to be admitted, I think about my mother. Finally I've found her, and she was, as I had hoped, one crazy lady.

For the first few years after she disappeared, my father and I were vigilant. With every phone call and doorbell ring, we expected her return. We would welcome her back with open arms. We would ask no questions and forgive all lies. We would bring on the celebrations, bring out the fatted calf. But it never happened. She never came back.

Dad left her clothes hanging in their bedroom closet, her make-up and perfumes on her dresser. He continued to renew her magazine subscriptions, letting the *Vogues* and *Good Housekeepings* pile up on the hall table month after month, year after year.

When he died from cirrhosis of the liver two years ago,

my brother Peter and I discovered that he had bought a double burial plot and a tombstone with my mother's name and birth date engraved next to his.

A nurse settles me into a wheelchair and pushes me on and off elevators, down a maze of corridors into a small green room. The contractions jar me out of my reverie. Clutching the sides of the wheelchair, I wince and pray for it to end now.

"Is someone coming to be with you?" another nurse asks as she takes my blood pressure and wipes my sweating brow.

Biting my lips so hard that they bleed, I shake my head and focus on my breathing. As each contraction sweeps through me, my mind wanders. Mother love. Mother Mary. Mother of God. Mother Teresa. Mother. Mom. Mama. Mummy.

Did she wonder about my brother and me?

Mommy dearest. Big mama. Mama's boy. Elvis's mom. Working mom. Stay-at-home mom. Single mom. Surrogate mom. No mom.

Does she think of me on my birthday?

I close my eyes and suck ice cubes. As contraction after contraction rolls through me, I cry out. I often told people she was dead. I wished she was.

And poor Peter. He was just a baby when she left. Now he's a father, married into a huge Italian family. The last time I saw him, his wife had just had bambino number three. After the christening, Peter threw his arms around me.

"You look more and more like mom every time I see you."

He babbled on about starting up the search again – classified ads, private detectives, even going on a talk show.

"Peter forget it," I said. "Forget her. You've got a wonderful family. She didn't and doesn't care about us. Pretend she's dead. That's what I do."

After dad died, I kept the photo album. There weren't many pictures and only a half dozen showed our mother. I spent hours studying them, searching for clues. Were her smiles false? Was her touch forced?

Oh cruel mama. You had such a pretty, smiling face. Your blue eyes sparkled on your wedding day, and sparkled again as you, pregnant with Peter, pushed me on the swing, two years before you left. Were those eyes glinting with love for us, or were you already harbouring your thoughts of escape?

You looked so happy in that Christmas picture, the last one in our photo album. You're sitting in front of the tree with Peter on your lap and me standing beside you. Peter's holding a teddy bear and I'm clutching my favourite doll, Nancy.

I've stared at that picture almost every day since dad died. It sits now in a black frame on my bedside table next to the alarm clock.

"Don't touch me," I scream as a nurse wipes my brow. I try to smile when Dr. Stern arrives, but as each contraction hits, I curse him.

"It won't be long now," he says, ignoring the abuse. "You're doing really well. I've called the Lanes. They're excited. They'll be here soon."

It was Dr. Stern who convinced me to have the baby. He told me about the Lanes and how hard they had tried to conceive. What good parents they would be.

Sweat pours down my face and mingles with my tears. I wipe my eyes and Dr. Stern is gone. A nurse comes in with more ice cubes. She babbles on about not remembering the pain afterwards and the first one being the hardest, but all I can think of are the Lanes.

Mary and Richard, so eager and so accommodating. Mary is about my age, fresh-faced, prim and pretty, a real Miss Goody Two-Shoes. And Richard with his pasted-on grin, looked like the accountant he is, dressed to impress in a blue suit and tie.

The nurse continues asking questions, not waiting for answers. I moan and she talks. I weep, she chatters on. I push, and at once people rush in shouting. They order me onto the stretcher and away we go down corridors and through doorways.

The pain rips and I scream. Then I push and push some more, and she slides out. Wailing, she's placed on my wet, heaving breast. I hold her tightly, as Dr. Stern presses my belly until my weary body expels the rest of her.

I'm in a bed when the Lanes come in, grinning like newlyweds and carrying bouquets of mums and carnations. The cloying smell reminds me of my father's casket. I clutch my baby and eye them warily.

Mary beams, "She's so tiny, so beautiful. Oh Richard, have you ever seen anything more precious?"

They're too close, almost on top of me. I can't breathe. I

thrust the baby at Mary and lurch from the bed to the bathroom. Closing the door, I turn on the taps and flush the toilet again and again.

"Hail Mary, Mother of God, help me. Help me."

I splash cold water on my face, my neck, my wrists. I breathe slowly in and out, in and out. I try counting. When I come out and crawl back into bed, Richard gingerly gives her to me.

"We can't thank you enough," he says. "Mary and I are so grateful. You should know you made the right decision. She will have a good life with us."

Later Dr. Stern brings the adoption papers. Without reading them, I sign and give my daughter away.

"In cases like this, I don't recommend breastfeeding," he says as I place Nancy at my swollen nipple. "It raises certain expectations on both sides. The nurses should have told you."

They had. But my breasts were sore and she found them and nuzzled and sucked whenever I held her. I hug her and hold her tight, letting her suck, all night long. As she drifts off to sleep, I tell her about my father and about her father and about her uncle Peter. I tell her that somewhere she has a grandma, and that I love her and always will.

I don't sleep that first and last night with my daughter. I stare at her face, at every part of her tiny perfect body. I try to memorize it all – the dark eyelashes, her sparkling brown eyes, the swirls of her ears, the oh-so-cute little nose, her fingernails and teensy toes, her wrinkled little feet that Mary Lane will be buying booties for.

The next morning, the nurse takes a Polaroid. She gives

me the picture and takes my baby.

I dress quickly and make my way down to ground level. Outside I walk a few blocks, not knowing what to do, where to go. When the tears start, I hail a cab and go to my apartment. There I slide her picture over my mother's in the black frame. My swollen breasts ache, and the pale milk seeps through my bra, staining my blouse with dark circles that radiate outward like two broken eggs.

House-Husband

He caught a glimpse of it out of the corner of his eye – a flash of red in the green bush. Putting down the paper, he quietly approached the patio door. There it was not 18 inches from him, a brilliant, fire-red cardinal hopping from branch to branch after gnats. He'd have to remember to tell Mary when she got home. He would have called the kids but knew they were no longer interested in bird-spotting. Where the hell were they anyway?

"Daniel, Katie, are you up? Your breakfast is waiting and this car leaves in 20 minutes."

"Katie won't get out of the bathroom," Daniel whined.

Five minutes later, Katie flounced down looking far too grown up for her 13 years.

"Your skirt's too short. Has your mother seen it on you?"

Katie blushed and grabbed a muffin.

"It's the same as everyone else's. Mom was with me

21

when I bought it."

As she sat next to him, the smell of *Je Reviens* brought Mary to mind. She used to wear that when they were first married. But perfume at school? He looked at Katie.

"What you starin' for pop-eyes?" she said and then sprinted down the hall to gather her books.

Daniel bounded into the kitchen, grabbed a bagel and flipped through the tech section of the paper.

"Got swimming today?"

Daniel grunted and continued to eat.

The seven block drive to West High was a treat he gave them – a hold-over from wintry and wet days, and a perk of his unemployment.

After dropping them off, he parked and lit a cigarette. He tried not to smoke around them, or at home, but could hardly wait for his first puff of the day. As he inhaled, he watched the teens hurrying into the building. A few, mostly girls, lingered around the door, talking and smoking.

Out of cigarettes, he drove to the 7-11. As he pulled into the parking lot, he saw her on the other side of the street. She looked like Katie. He thought she was waiting to cross but she was still standing there when he came out of the store. He stared as he lit his second smoke of the day. She looked kind of lost. Maybe her ride to school didn't show. He glanced at his watch. After 9. She was late.

"Need a lift?" he called.

She pranced across the street almost getting hit and setting off a cacophony of horns. Up close he saw how tight her red leather mini skirt was, how smudged her eyes.

"Late for school?"

"Sure," she giggled, "and I guess you're the teach rounding up tardy students."

As she got into the seat next to him, he noticed her skirt riding up her thighs, her breasts falling out of her t-shirt. Before he could ask her which school she was late for, she said, "It's $60 for a blow job. If you want more it'll cost you and you pay for the place."

His mouth dropped open. He cleared his throat.

"$60's it. I don't do it for less, so whadya say — yes or no? Hurry up or I'm outta here. Payment up front."

"But," he said as he butted his cigarette in the ashtray, "I just wanted to help you. You reminded me of someone. I thought you needed a ride."

"Yeah, well you're mistaken pops. We got a deal or not?" Her hand reached for the door handle.

"Wait."

He pulled three twenties from his pocket and handed them to her.

"Let's talk a bit."

"Whatever you want," she said tucking the bills into her purse. "We can go to the park behind the restaurant."

He glanced at her, his hands clammy, sweat forming on his forehead.

"I think I've made a mistake."

He was finding it hard to breathe. She chewed gum, stared out the window, and said nothing.

"I'll drive you back — you can keep the money."

"I know, I know. You've never done this before," she

said rubbing her nose. "You're a faithful husband in a happy marriage. You don't have to explain. It just wastes air. There's the restaurant. You can park in the back."

"But I really can't."

He drove past the restaurant and down into the valley below. At the stop sign, two joggers in bright red track suits sprinted by. An old man was walking his collie.

"Suit yourself, but pick a place soon or it'll cost you more."

"Look," he said, leaning towards her, "why not come back to my place? We can talk there."

She shrugged, and he drove home. He dropped the keys when he tried to open the back door quickly and as he flung the door open, the cat ran out.

"Damn it. Gotta get him."

He pushed her into the kitchen.

"I'll be right in."

Usually Tiger just lay down and rolled when he got out, but today he leaped over the fence and into the Bartle's yard.

By the time he grabbed the cat and got back into the house, he'd lost her. Walking anxiously from room to room, he realized he didn't even know her name. He found her examining the family photos on the mantle in the living room.

"Is this your daughter? She's a looker."

He grabbed the photo out of her hands.

"Look, I really did pick you up by mistake. I didn't realize you were – working."

"Shush, don't worry. I'm very good and I'll make you

feel really good, too. You picked right this time."

Taking his hand, she led him to Mary's chair next to the fireplace. Moistening her lips and smiling, she pushed him into the chair and kneeled before him. He felt nauseous and closed his eyes. A few minutes later, she wiped her mouth on his pant leg then hurried into the kitchen.

"Getting a Coke," she called back to him. "You want one?"

He opened his eyes, looked down at his unzipped pants and swore.

"You sure got a lot of stuff," she said when she came back sipping a Coke. "Are you some sort of collector?"

Before he could answer, the doorbell rang. Zipping his pants, and wiping his face on his shirt sleeve, he hurried to the door. Canvassing for cancer. He handed over a twenty, swaying from foot to foot as he waited for a receipt.

Back in the living room, he gasped. She lay on the couch with a devil's mask covering her face.

"This would be great for Hallowe'en."

He tore the mask off and hung it back on the wall.

"Okay, let's go. I'll drive you back."

"Cool it man – I'm not hurting your precious things. Just wanna have some fun."

He pushed her toward the car.

"It's the same with all you old farts. Once you got it, it's outta here bitch. Gimme a cigarette, dude."

He threw the pack at her.

"Shut up and just get in the car."

Back home, he flung open the windows and took a

steamy hot shower, scrubbed down the bathroom and sprayed the whole house with Lysol. With the towel still wrapped around him like a sarong, he poured himself a scotch and sat on the living room couch facing Mary's chair.

What the fuck have I done? Downing one drink and then another, he flicked on CNN. As images of atrocities brutalized the screen, his head flopped forward. When the front door slammed, he jerked awake, spilling scotch on his naked chest.

Later, he picked on Katie during supper until she fled in tears to her room.

"Is something wrong honey?" Mary asked.

"I don't think she should dress like a hooker," he said, "and she should show us some respect."

Getting up from the table, he added, "I've got work to do. Don't wait up. You can go to bed without me."

After dropping Daniel and Katie off the next morning, he returned to the 7-11. She was there. Same tight red skirt. Another car slowed down.

He rolled down his window and called, "Hey, got a minute? Come on over and get warm."

She ran across the street and hopped into his car.

"I knew you'd be back," she laughed as she took a long drag on the cigarette he handed her.

"I just wanted to explain," he began but stopped as she bent over and caressed his crotch.

"It's okay. You've been bad, but that's good, you know."

She was so sassy, but God it felt good, her long blond hair tickling him as she sucked. Mary had got her hair cut a week after they got married and had kept it short since. That night at supper when Katie told her brother to fuck off, he slapped her across the face.

"Clean up your mouth, you talk like a slut."

"What's got into you? Have you gone crazy?" Mary said checking to see that Katie was okay. "All the kids talk like that. You didn't have to hit her."

The next morning, Katie, wearing a tight red mini skirt, refused the ride to school.

After dropping Daniel off, he went to the 7-11. She wasn't there. He bought a coffee and sat in his car smoking and waiting. She didn't appear. He went home, but couldn't settle down. He got in the car and went back to the 7-11. Still no sign of her.

After supper that night, he went to pick up a jug of milk. He thought he saw her on the corner. But when he stopped the car close to the curb, he realized it wasn't her. The hooker smiled as she approached the car and he sped off.

He pulled into the driveway and walked around the side of the house. He sat in the backyard gazebo and gazed skyward. There were no stars, no moon. A bank of clouds covered the sky from east to west. Looking toward the house, he saw lights on in every room. In the kitchen, the curtains were wide open and he saw Mary sitting at the table, reading and having a cup of tea. Tiger was at the window in Daniel's room, where the eerie glow of the computer lit up the ceiling. In Katie's room the shades were pulled down tight but he could see her shadow, gracefully flitting back and forth as she danced to music he could not hear.

Solitaire

We never visited grandpa much. Mom said he didn't like people and preferred to be alone. She also said to dad, when she thought we weren't listening, that she didn't like him much either.

"Never did, never will," she said.

Sometimes when we were passing through the town where she was born, we'd make a pit stop at grandpa's. Dad would always offer to wait in the car but mom said he'd better come up or it wouldn't look good.

"We'll only stay a few minutes, say hi and use the bathroom," she said.

The visits were fast. We'd hardly get our shoes off and put the TV on low so it wouldn't bother grandpa, and mom would say, "Well, we'd better go before it gets dark. You know how I hate driving in the dark."

Grandpa would offer us ginger ale and cookies, but he'd never speak directly to us. "They want something?" he'd say.

Or "Kids are getting tall."

Sometimes he'd stop playing cards and turn off the radio when we were there. Mom would make tea and ask him if he'd won the lottery yet.

"No fuckin' chance of that," he'd say and laugh and cough at the same time.

Mom would ask about his health and then talk about the weather.

If she mentioned grandma, he'd say, "She's better off in the ground. I'd be better off fuckin' dead too."

We'd go pretty soon after that and wouldn't see him for months afterwards.

One weekend though, mom and dad had to go to a wedding in her hometown. Jeff, my kid brother, was staying with his best friend for the weekend so they were leaving me with grandpa for the day.

I didn't mind as much as I let them think I did. I had my DS and could always watch TV. The screen was small but at least I wouldn't have to fight Jeff over what to watch. I figured grandpa would just play cards and sleep. And I wasn't much mistaken.

When I first got there he was sitting at the dining room table shuffling cards and laying them out. Classical music played low on the radio. I sat next to him and watched.

Six of hearts on the seven of spades. Jack of diamonds on the queen of clubs. Ace of hearts out. A red king, then a black.

"Damn, no space," he said.

I moved onto the sofa and pulled out my DS.

A few minutes later, I heard him say, "Fourteen. No damn good. No luck today."

Then he stacked the cards in a pile, pushed his chair back, farted and went into the kitchen.

"Want a drink?" he asked as he thrust a glass into my hand. "Apple juice and ginger ale. It's good. Lots of Vitamin C. Keep you regular, too."

Grandpa drank his down in one gulp, then burped loudly. He rinsed the glass out and put it on the dish rack.

"I gotta rest now," he said as he lay down on his never-made bed. "I need my strength and a clear head to pick the numbers. Maybe you'll bring me luck."

On Wednesdays and Saturdays, he brought his lottery numbers to the 7-11 across the street from his apartment building. Buying lottery tickets and shopping for food at the store a block away were the extent of his outings most days.

He cooked for himself but without enthusiasm. His food was boring. I remember mostly meat — goulash soup, stewed chicken wings and pork chops. But there were always lots of goodies. Cookies, cakes and donuts filled the cupboard next to the sink.

Mom said that he'd gotten a sweet tooth when he quit drinking.

"He doesn't seem to have put on weight from that sweet junk though," she said. "He's thinner now than when he was first married."

The phone rarely rang at grandpa's. Still to make sure he wasn't bothered by wrong numbers, he unplugged it at night and often forgot to plug it back in.

As for friends, mom said he had none and she wasn't surprised. He'd lost touch with his drinking buddies when he had a heart attack and quit the steel company years ago.

Sometimes he'd run into his neighbours, mostly old women who lived in the building.

"They're all real friendly to me," he'd say after an encounter in the laundry room.

"Wore out their fuckin' husbands, now they're after me."

"I had enough listening to her aches and pains," he'd say about grandma. "Not going to make that mistake again."

After a few hours of DS and a TV that didn't have cable, I was seriously bored. Grandpa was asleep so I rummaged around the bookcase. All I could find were an encyclopedia, stacks of *Reader's Digest* magazines, needlepoint books, an atlas and a couple of old sci-fi paperbacks.

A small leather suitcase took up half of the bottom shelf. It wasn't locked so I opened it. It was full of pictures. There was mom when she was a baby. We had the same picture in our photo album at home. And there was grandma and grandpa on their wedding day. We had that one in a frame on the upstairs hall table. There were photos of me and my brother as babies, and all of our stupid school pictures.

But most of the pictures didn't look familiar at all and a lot were black and white. Some were really old, yellow, stained and cracked.

I started to arrange them in piles according to who looked like they belonged together. Before too long, I had about eight sets. I had gotten so caught up in my sorting that I jumped and dropped a pile when I heard grandpa cough right behind me.

"Nobody's touched them pictures since she died. She was always looking at them too. Not me, I never wanted to see them. Should have thrown the whole fuckin' lot in the garbage."

"I was just kinda bored," I said and started to put the piles back in the suitcase.

Then I saw him staring at a picture of two boys. Both were wearing old-fashioned suits and smiling. A fake backdrop made it look as though they were on an old-time movie set.

Grandpa picked the picture up.

"Where's your brother today? He could have come to visit, too," he said. "Although your mother doesn't think so, I wouldn't have eaten him."

"He's staying with his friend for the weekend."

"You like your brother?" he said, still looking at the picture.

I shrugged.

"Sure, he's okay for a kid."

I wondered why I was getting the third degree.

Grandpa placed the picture face up on the table as though it was a playing card and picked up another from the same pile. It showed the two boys again. In this picture, the younger one was wearing a uniform, grinning and pointing his gun at the other boy. Grandpa placed it next to the other one. Soon, he had the whole pile spread out on the table in front of him.

"Who are those guys?" I asked.

"Don't you recognize me?" he said pointing at the older of the pair. "And that's my kid brother, Laszlo. You never knew him. He died long before you were born. Always a joker, always happy. He got his last laugh in the fuckin' war. Just a kid."

After that grandpa was quiet for a long time just staring at the pictures of him and his brother. When he got up to put some music on the tape deck, I thought I'd better put the pictures away before he started talking again.

I spent the rest of the day watching TV while grandpa lay on his bed. I sure was glad when mom finally buzzed and called me to come down. Grandpa got up to shake my hand and told me to be good and look after my brother.

"Remember he's just a kid," he said.

I'd completely forgotten the visit until two weeks later when a letter came addressed to me in the mail.

Michael, grandpa wrote, Laszlo and I used to collect stamps. I found these and thought you and Jeff might like to start a collection. If you like, I can send you more.

Love Envies No One

The stone in my ring fell out today
I wrapped it in tissue
and placed it
and the ring
in the drawer of my memories.

Running up the concrete steps of the grand Romanesque church, I heard the final strands of *Ode to Joy* and knew I was late. Ignoring the ushers, I pushed my way to a pew on the bride's side about seven rows from the front and squeezed next to the guests.

I hardly had a chance to catch my breath and straighten my hat when the strains of the *Wedding March* filled the church and the wedding party began their precisely-paced stroll down the aisle.

I settled back to watch the white-tuxedoed ushers and purple-gowned bridesmaids in perfect height order make their way past my pew. Two tiny flower girls and a dimple-faced ring-bearer followed the graceful maid of honour.

This seems to be a good choice – a traditional formal wedding. I've been craving one all week ever since last week's new age disaster.

All that previous Saturday afternoon had been wasted. Everything about that wedding – from the tasteless multi-coloured dress that the bride had worn to the female deacon who conducted the ceremony – was so wrong. And in all the blathering about the cosmos and mother earth, I almost missed the exchange of vows which turned out to be unsuitable as well, emphasizing the couple's joined but parallel lives. Each of them had promised to cherish their separate pasts and not to smother each other's existence in the future.

What bunk! They're just setting themselves up for an easy exit when the going gets rough or worse, a lifetime of lazy companionship.

The bridal chorus broke my train of thought and I gasped as I caught sight of today's bride. Under the veil, she seemed to be a natural honey blonde just like me. She was also my height. Her gown, a flattering princess-line style in ice white satin embroidered with a small rosebud motif, looked like my wedding dress. Although mine was nearly seven years old now and quite unseemly to my newly single situation, I still kept it wrapped in yards of tissue at the bottom of my cedar hope chest.

The minister's baritone voice echoed through the church as he intoned the traditional opening words.

"If marriage is to last a lifetime," he declared, "it must be built upon love."

I trembled knowing what was to follow.

"Let me share with you," he said, "a beautiful description from the apostle Paul to the Corinthians of what it takes to build a happy home."

I began to choke up as I heard the words that I chanted every night while struggling to fall asleep.

"Love is patient; love is kind and envies no one. Love is never boastful, nor conceited, nor rude; never selfish, not quick to take offense…"

I had never been in this high Anglican church before today, yet the words reverberating in my mind were the same familiar tune I'd heard at wedding after wedding. And God knows I'd been to enough weddings in the last few months.

"Love keeps no score of wrongs; does not gloat over other men's sins, but delights in the truth. There is nothing love cannot face; there is no limit to its faith, its hope and its endurance."

No score of wrongs. I laughed. Let me count the wrongs.

People on both sides glanced reprovingly at me as today's bride slowly lifted the veil that protected her from evil spirits. The exchange of vows, my favourite part, had begun.

"Will you promise to love, honour, trust and serve her in sickness and in health, in adversity and prosperity, and to be true and loyal to her, so long as you both shall live?"

"I will," the groom said loudly.

Then the bride whispered her agreement.

The words of empty promise never failed to twist my insides no matter how many times I heard them. Every time someone marries, my heart bleeds.

As the exchange of rings took place, my pain intensified and I wove a silent curse on them both: *Words too soon will be forgotten and you too will wake up one fine sunny morn and wonder why.*

"Our prayer," said the minister, "is that your love for each other will be as eternal and everlasting as these rings. Jeff, do you give this ring to Pam as a token of your love for her?"

Jeff and Pam – names for innocent, foolish children.

"...to love and to cherish 'til death do us part."

I doubt Jeff and Pam that your names will be together on your tombstones.

"And with this ring I pledge thee my love."

A diamond-studded band. How typical and so ostentatious, just like the entire ceremony.

I felt my bare ring finger and smiled knowingly. A diamond with all its sparkling brilliance was supposed to last forever, but more likely than not, it would be lost or stolen.

Remember Jeff and Pam that diamonds, the hardest and most imperishable of all stones, come from the earth and to the earth you both will go – separately, I'm sure.

"What therefore God has joined together, let no man put asunder."

No woman either, I thought remembering another wedding where those same words had struck me like a thunderbolt.

Back then the Mass had lulled me into a kind of meditative trance when the words struck. A stream of words so powerful I wanted to scream. Scream and destroy the very tableaux in front of me. Scream and destroy not just them but also myself for all my grievous sins past, present, and to come. Mea culpa, mea culpa, mea maxima culpa.

Now with great fanfare the wedding march boomed through the church. The wedding party, led by Jeff and Pam, practically danced down the aisle and into the sunshine.

I scuttled past the guests to watch the bride, train in hand, prepare to throw her bouquet. Standing to one side, I ducked to avoid the sacred rice being showered on the wedding party.

No rice will appease this evil spirit. A year from now Pam, your cheeks won't be glowing pink from happiness, your eyes won't be sparkling in anticipation of untold joys. I think for you Pam, there will be many tears and much misery.

With this final silent declaration, I raised my hands to carve the arcane symbols of my curse in the air, but instead found the hated thing of flowers and lace, suddenly, irrefutably, in my hands.

Sultan of the Sidewalk

He was big for a beggar, brawny under all the tattered blankets. Maybe he was new at it. Sitting cross-legged like some sultan of the sidewalk, you couldn't miss him. Although he occupied only the north-east corner of King and Bay, his presence dominated the entire intersection.

His head, topped by a ragged Montreal-Canadiens toque, slumped forward onto his chest. But the icy blasts of sleet and snow that howled through the financial district ensured that he never slept. His sandbagged eyes were vigilant, observing the relentless scurrying of office workers, stockbrokers and financiers.

From ground level he saw, as few do, the cold underbelly of the city – the winter-grimed cars spewing exhaust fumes, the diesel buses lurching to a halt to pick up and drop off load after load of work-weary commuters, and the daredevil bike couriers wheeling up over the curbs through red lights and green, weaving between pedestrians and around cabs.

The beggar's red and raw fingers were wrapped around a battered, nearly empty cookie tin. Unlike the city hall freeloader who greeted one and all with an ebullient, "If it pleases you, a loonie for a coffee. Thank you kindly." or the foul-mouthed group of drunks permanently installed outside the liquor store, this wretched man sat like a penitent outside some Latin American church faithfully observing his vow of silence. A coin, dropped noisily into his tin can, brought forth no words of thanks, only a slight, almost disdainful nod of acknowledgement.

I first saw him on an icy November day as Marsha, Sandy and I struggled out of a cab after a client meeting. Instead of pocketing the change from the trip, I tossed it to the beggar.

My cursory action didn't go unnoticed. Marsha nudged Sandy and they both laughed.

"Paul's got so much moola he can throw it away," Sandy said.

"No," said Marsha, "Paul's just taking out some insurance on this campaign. Protection money, right?"

I laughed. Marsha could read me like an open book. We had started out in retail together years ago, struggling to make the ad agency big time. From the beginning, she helped me create great campaigns. Marsha knew that I'd screw my own mother to bag a client, or win an award. Not for me the day-to-day administrative paperwork. I knew where the big bucks and the glory lay and that's where I wanted to be.

On my way to a client lunch a few days later, I passed

the beggar again. He looked as if he hadn't moved, frozen to the spot. But surely, I thought, he must go home to sleep at night. I flicked a loonie at him and moved on.

While lunching at the trendy Down and Out Grill, I found myself briefly wondering how that beggar would feel about paying $14 for a bowl of designer chili and toast, or $12 for macaroni and cheese.

That evening after work, I made a point of walking by King and Bay. He was gone. The corner looked deserted.

In the night I dreamt about tossing him a few coins. Only this time he looked straight up at me and started to yell "It's not enough. You've got lots. Give me more." Then he leapt up, threw off his blankets and, with a demented look, lumbered toward me. As he grabbed me, his face morphed into my own and I woke to the sound of *All You Need is Love* on the clock radio.

Being creative director for a hot-shop ad agency meant that I could come and go as I pleased. It wasn't unusual for me, when struggling to find a solution to a client's problem, to disappear from the office for hours at a time. This is what I started to do. Only I wasn't solving any problems or having any brilliant insights, I just watched the beggar on Bay.

I walked by his corner several times a day. To be certain that he wouldn't notice me, I kept my distance, dropping coins in his can only once in a while. I found a hallway with a large window on the second floor of an office building across the street from him. There I could loiter inconspicuously and watch him in warmth and relative comfort. Over a week I certainly learned a lot about the habits of one local beggar.

He arrived on foot from the east end at 8:30 in the morning, spread newspapers and a piece of cardboard on the sidewalk, then with great dignity, sat down on them, pulling his blankets close.

He sat almost motionless until 11 when he got up, emptied the contents of the tin can into his pants pocket and dismantled his seating arrangement. He carefully placed the paper, cardboard, blankets and tin can behind a nearby garbage container. Slowly and stiffly, he then walked north.

One day, I followed at a distance and waited outside while he used the john at the bus terminal. At the take-out, he bought a sausage on a bun and ate it as he shuffled back down to his corner. There he retrieved his stuff and set himself up for the lunch crowd.

At 2:30 he repeated his morning routine, returning to his spot by 3:30 when workers streamed out of the office towers. At 6:30, he walked east to the Good Shepherd Shelter.

I was amazed at how organized and methodical his day was – how similar to my own working day. It also worried me that I had spent the day stalking a beggar. Was it fear that made me follow him? If it weren't for the next successful campaign, and the one after that, and the one after that, like an endless loop, could I end up as a beggar on Bay street?

Ridiculous! I may not have been the top creative director in the city yet, but I was damn good and had all the perks to show for it: my penthouse condo overlooking the lake, a green Jag XKE, trips to New Orleans at Mardi Gras, skiing at Whistler, jetting to Paris and London whenever I felt the urge. I knew I could never end up like that beggar.

Yet I felt there was something about him. Something I wanted; something I needed. After a week of observation, I knew I had to talk to him. As if this wasn't weird enough, I was actually nervous about it. The dream that I'd had earlier – would it come true?

After a night of tossing and turning, I resolved to do it.

I pulled a twenty from my wallet, removed my gloves and walked up to him. I hesitated a second, then bent over and instead of dropping the bill into his cookie tin, I grasped his hard and frozen hand and slid the bill into it.

A small, pinched smile broke his cracked lips.

"Thank you sir," he said, coughing slightly.

I did not move on.

"How about a coffee?" I said. "I'd like to talk to you."

"Hey man, I'm not bothering anyone. What are you a fuckin' cop? Here, take your lousy money."

He threw the twenty back at me.

"I just thought you might like to warm up," I said, picking the bill off the ground and putting it into his can.

Then I quickly walked away.

What did I expect? Did I think I was a new age Messiah, a Father Teresa for Christ's sake? What did I hope to gain from talking to him anyway? A friendly chat over coffee? Oh yeah!

But I realized I did want something from him. Something I once had and something I still needed to keep my edge in the business. I needed his unsullied perspective on things. His experience as the ultimate outsider in the city, the proverbial man-in-the-street. Like some monk of old, he must have a vast storehouse of knowledge that I could use.

When I told Marsha what I'd been doing, she rolled her eyes.

"Well Paul, I always knew you were a mercenary. But I think you've sunk to a new low. The poor bugger won't have a chance once you start on him."

The next day I walked with him up Bay to the bus terminal. I talked non-stop, apologized for upsetting him the day before, told him I wasn't a cop but in advertising, and pleaded with him to trust me. We pissed side by side at the urinals in the bus terminal and I paid for his sausage and coffee.

I convinced him to come home with me that night. After supper and a hot shower, we talked. I found out his name was Jim. He was a laid off construction worker, had a wife and kids in the suburbs and just couldn't handle it once his unemployment insurance ran out. He'd been on the streets for about a year and saw no end in sight. He wasn't a brilliant conversationalist but he did have a storehouse of stories about life on the street. I didn't take notes but I recorded it all.

The next day, I gave him a hundred bucks and dropped him off at his downtown spot. Got that monkey off my back.

About a week later, I went to a gallery to see photos taken for the internationally acclaimed Benetton campaign. I was stunned by these breathtakingly memorable slice of life images that had done wonders for Benetton's stock.

Then I thought of the boring RRSP ad campaign that was giving Marsha and me trouble. I smiled. A new campaign played out in front of my eyes. I'd cut from a collage of shots of what retirement would be like if you invested with Country-Wide Trust — fishing from a yacht, strolling on a beach, dining in an elegant restaurant — to zoom into the gritty reality of a spot waiting for you at King and Bay if you failed to save for retirement.

To really impress the client with my creativity, I'd present not just mock-ups but the actual star of the campaign. It was brilliant. They'd eat it up.

The bankers were a bit taken aback when I walked into their boardroom with Beggar Jim in tow. But my brilliant strategy and creative rationale, coupled with the resounding success of my last campaign for them, easily won them over.

Jim joined the actors' union and soon got used to the klieg lights, backdrops and lavish lifestyle rampant on any shoot. When I saw him, drink in hand, chatting up Katie, my bubbly production assistant or having an intimate talk over sushi with Marsha, I figured he'd crawled out of his depressing hole for good. Once the commercials were in the can and the stills all taken for the print campaign, it was time to pay him off and send him on his way.

With the money he made, I thought he'd head home and try to get his life together. I heard though that he squandered all his earnings on lottery tickets. Go figure.

Soon he was back at his spot on Bay. But once the commercials aired, he could no longer make it as a beggar. Passersby would stop and ask him if he was the RRSP guy. He'd nod and they'd move on, unwilling to toss this actor a cent.

I got a few voice messages from him asking if I had any leads on a job, but never returned his calls. Marsha tried to get him in as a gopher with a film crew but that never panned out.

Not long after that, Marsha and I seemed to lose our rapport. That campaign turned out to be the last one we worked on together. The commercials though struck the zeitgeist and won awards in every category. For a while, I became the most in-demand creative director in the city. I accepted a VP position with Samuels and Carnale, moved uptown and avoided King and Bay like the plague.

The Good Wife

My mother was in her Shogun period when I got married.

"I know you're going ahead with it," she said. "I've told you how I feel so I'm not going to repeat myself, but I'd like to give you this."

She handed me a black lacquered box with an ornate clasp. Inside was a slender silver dagger lying on a bed of purple velvet. Its cherry wood handle was intricately carved with a series of overlapping circles.

"What's this for?" I said as I gingerly examined it.

Mom smiled.

"It's a traditional Japanese wedding gift bestowed by the mother of the bride on her daughter. A reminder not to come home crying to mommy if you're having marital problems. If the marriage fails, the bride is to use the dagger – on herself."

"How awful!" I said throwing the dagger on the bed.

"Don't be silly," she said giving me a hug. "It's a

beautiful treasure and symbolic. It's to remind you to be a good wife and over the years, you'll see, all wives could use a reminder."

Mom put the dagger reverently back into its coffin-shaped box and tucked it into my handbag.

"Geez mom, you are really weird."

I fixed my make-up and we went off to my bridal shower arm-in-arm giggling like two school girls sharing a wicked secret.

My mother never mentioned her gift again and I never spoke about it either. I kept it in the top drawer of my dresser, hidden under my bras and panties.

Jeff and I had lived together for six months before tying the knot. I can't remember whose idea it was to get married, or why. But marriage seemed to be in the air that spring. A number of our friends were getting hitched, so we did too.

We had a storybook wedding in June with one hundred and fifty guests attending a garden ceremony and lavish reception at the country club. Following it was an idyllic honeymoon in Paris where we did all the touristy things – climbed to the top of the Eiffel Tower, cruised down the Seine and visited the Folies Bergere. It was every girl's fantasy come true.

I was madly in love with Jeff. He was tall, handsome and charming; ambitious and success driven. He also liked the same things I did – movies and theatre, gourmet cooking and travel.

From the beginning though my mother didn't like him.

"I don't trust him. He's too nice," she said after first

meeting him. Her sign-off to every conversation with me was "Be careful love."

The first months of our marriage were a whirlwind of activities. We went out to movies, theatre and dinner almost every night. Both our jobs, Jeff's as a sales rep for a computer company and mine as a make-up artist, were exciting and fast-paced. We thrived on meeting impossible deadlines at work and came together to talk and drink after hours and on weekends. Our time together was romantic, playful, and hot.

Then, without warning, Jeff hit me. I was dumbfounded.

We had been to see a movie, a romantic comedy, and went for a few drinks and a bite to eat at the pub around the corner from where we lived. Suddenly Jeff wanted to leave right away.

"Can I just finish my drink?" I said as he threw some bills on the table.

"No way bitch," he said quietly.

"But Jeff what's wrong?"

I grabbed my leather jacket and followed him out the door. As soon as we got outside, he turned and slapped me across the face.

"Don't talk back to me ever again."

I stared in shock as he walked away.

When I got home, I found him sprawled across our big brass bed. He was fully clothed and snoring loudly.

I took a pillow and blanket from the closet and spent the night fitfully sleeping on the sofa in the living room. I re-hashed the evening from beginning to end but could find no reason for Jeff to hit me.

I awoke to his kisses and tears as he gently stroked my hair and face.

"I'm so sorry sweetheart. Please forgive me. I don't know what got into me. I'll never do it again."

I hugged him and began to cry too.

"You just had a bad day," I said wiping away his tears and my own. "And too much to drink. We both did. Of course I forgive you. I'm your wife."

Like a child, he wouldn't let up until I reassured him repeatedly. Then he took me on the sofa in such a sweet and tender way that I swear the earth moved. We never mentioned the incident again.

So I was just as surprised, when a few months later, he began hitting and punching me for no reason. I fought back and broke my arm in the struggle.

At the hospital Jeff comforted and coddled me. He smiled when I told the nurse, and later the doctor, that I had fallen off a chair while changing a light bulb.

Afterwards at home I tried to discuss what had happened.

"Honey, you're making too big a deal of it," he said laughing. "Anyone could fall off a chair."

Then kissing and stroking me ever so gently, he whispered in my ear, "I love you so much but sometimes you make me lose all sense of control. I can't help myself. You drive me crazy."

From then on he slapped me almost every night. I realized that if I didn't struggle, his blows turned into loving caresses sooner.

I stopped going to work when I ran out of excuses for the bruises which even my make-up wizardry couldn't always hide. Jeff didn't mind me quitting. He said he preferred his wife to be home where she could look after her husband. Besides his career was skyrocketing.

Often alone in the house, I would take my mother's wedding gift out of its box and examine it closely. The handle of the dagger became warmer the longer I held it. I would turn it round and round in my one hand while the fingers of my other hand slipped easily up and down and over the blade. Sometimes hours would pass as I sat fondling it and thinking about Jeff and whether I was a good wife.

One day, startled out of my reverie by the phone ringing, I was surprised to see a few drops of blood from my ring finger on my white bathrobe.

My younger sister thought that I really lucked out when I married Jeff.

After I told her that he hit me, she said, "Just remember Cathy, you made your bed and believe me with a guy like Jeff, if you won't lie in it, someone else will. Besides a little rough stuff can be a super turn-on, don't you think?"

I couldn't answer because I knew she was right. Making out with Jeff after he hit me felt so good and always made everything all right again.

I had lunch with Marg, a hairdresser at the salon where I'd worked. She noticed a particularly bad bruise on my cheek. After a second glass of wine, I told her what was happening.

"Get out of it before it's too late Cathy," she said. "Just

move on. Get a divorce. You're still young. You'll find someone who won't hurt you."

I promised her that I would find a lawyer, all the while knowing I wouldn't. I couldn't consider divorce. It was a sin. Besides I was a Scorpio – marriage for better or worse was for life. And I really loved Jeff. When he was good, he was very, very good.

Most days I closed the blinds and soaked in a rose-scented bath to soothe my bruised body and calm my confused mind. I inhaled musky incense, lit votive candles and stared at the dagger propped on the edge of the bathtub.

Dried off, I lay naked on our bed dragging it gently over my whole body, all the while murmuring nonsense rhymes.

One two, buckle my shoe. Three four, close the door. Five six, pick up sticks.

Sometimes the dagger would get so hot and damp, it would slip from my grasp, nicking me as it fell onto the floor.

By the time Jeff came home, the dagger was safely back in its box. And I was calm and loving, a good wife servicing her husband after his labours.

When I got pregnant, Jeff stopped hitting me. He seemed fascinated with the changes my body was going through and loved putting his head on my belly to feel any movements inside me. We decorated his man cave in Disney prints, started buying baby things, and signed up for pre-natal classes.

My mother brought out her knitting needles when she heard the news.

"Girl or boy," she said, "you'll have to be careful Cathy.

Watch out for Jeff."

I was in my seventh month and sound asleep on my back when Jeff punched me in the face. I screamed as I saw his foot take aim at my belly and turned towards the wall just in time. He kicked me hard several times and then left.

I spent the night alone and it wasn't until noon the next day that I could move my aching body off the bed. I sighed with relief to feel the baby still moving inside me. As I soaked away the pain in the tub, I wondered what I had done to cause Jeff to hurt me so. Then I noticed the bathwater turning pink.

At the hospital I told them I had fallen in the tub and started bleeding. The ER doctor prescribed immediate bed rest to avert a miscarriage.

Jeff came home that night with red roses and take-out Chinese food. He begged my forgiveness and cried when I told him what the doctor had said. He swore he would never hurt me again.

Through all his professions of love and pleadings for forgiveness, I lay mute in bed clasping both my hands over my belly. I could feel the baby's frequent kicks and when Jeff lay his head on my belly, I let him, so he could feel the kicks too. So he wouldn't hurt us again.

Soon he fell asleep, but I lay awake watching the play of light and shadows on the wall.

In the morning after he'd gone to work, I took the dagger from its box. The sun streaming in from the window glinted on its silver blade. I was transfixed by its radiance. Then I heard a bell pealing. The mournful dirge came closer until I recognized its source. The tool sharpener with his whetstone was making his way to my front door. I pulled on a dress and hurried out. The dagger needed sharpening.

Robbery in Rome

Christopher Miles, his slender hands folded on his lap, was waiting in a small room at the central police station on via S. Vitale in Rome when he heard heavy footsteps coming down the hallway.

Doc Marten's, he thought, American, male.

As a bearded man pushed open the door, Christopher smiled to himself. The man hesitated in the doorway, surveying the room. He reached into his leather jacket and pulled out a Berlitz "Italian for Travellers".

A grin crept across Christopher's face as he watched this aging hipster fumble through the pages of the small book only to stammer excitedly, "Mi scusi, parla inglese? I've been robbed."

"You too, eh." Christopher sighed and shook his head. "Bloody thieves broke into my room this morning while I was at the market. My landlady, of course, didn't hear or see anything."

"Thank goodness you speak English," the man said. He tucked the Berlitz book into his pocket and continued.

"Name's Harold. They smashed in my car window, tore out the stereo and, as if that wasn't enough, they slashed the seats, back and front — absolutely ruined."

He sat down heavily and put his head in his hands.

"That's a shame," Christopher said, not really certain this guy had much cause to be so upset. It was after all only a car.

"It's not so much the cost, the insurance should cover that," Harold said as if reading Christopher's thoughts. "But what kind of maniac, after taking the stereo — I mean that's what he must have wanted — what kind of crazy would just hack the hell out of the leather upholstery? For what reason?"

"Same kind of person who would take a knife to a da Vinci, I guess," Christopher said. Then he asked politely, "The car new?"

"My wife and I just bought it in Sweden a month ago. A Volvo. We decided to take a trip before shipping it back to the States. The difference in price more than pays for our vacation."

They both turned towards the door as a burly man in a rumpled business suit rushed in. He glanced at them and said, "I want to report a robbery."

Christopher smirked.

"The inspector won't be back from lunch until four o'clock. Siesta, you know."

"Four o'clock," the man shouted. "Damn. By then, what hope will they have of finding the thieves. I tried to chase them but I'm not so young anymore."

He wiped his sweating brow with a hanky before sitting down.

"Besides," he said, "they were on a motorcycle. Two of them. One steering while the other grabbed my briefcase as I was walking down the street. Before I realized it, they had weaved through the traffic. No one stopped them."

"What a system," Harold said, "That makes three of us robbed in one morning. They must like foreigners. What did they get?"

"My passport and all my work papers. Can't do anything without them," he said angrily. "Not even worth much to them."

"I don't think that matters to this kind of thief," Christopher said. "He stole my laptop, which of course, he can sell. But I can't figure out why he would take my journal. It's absolutely useless to anyone but me."

Each man retreated into silence, lulled by the heat of the afternoon and disconsolate over their personal losses. Their mutual grief was interrupted when a handsome, elegantly tailored man weeping copiously walked through the door.

Embarrassed, they glanced at the stranger, then at one another.

Christopher said wryly, "The tourist brochures never said anything about it, but it looks like being robbed is part of the package deal here."

"What did they get from you?" Harold asked the newcomer.

The stranger pulled out a silk handkerchief, blew his

nose noisily and looked at them with such sadness that they knew their losses were light compared to his tragedy.

"My camera equipment," he sobbed with a thick Italian accent. "Thousands of dollars worth. My career is finished," he said before bursting into a new flood of tears.

"It's not the end of the world," Harold said. "The police might be able to catch the thieves and recover our things."

"Ha," shouted the photographer, "you do not know the Italian police. I don't even know why I am here. You will see. The police are useless. You will wait and wait, and then they will make you fill out pages and pages of forms in no less than 20 copies. And that's it. Gone forever. Unless…."

He stopped and slowly lit a cigarette.

"Never mind," he said suddenly, dragging long on his cigarette. "I see it is siesta time for the carabinieri, so I must go and play private detective. Maybe I will be lucky. Otherwise," he shrugged his shoulders, "I am ruined."

"Wait a minute," said Christopher, thinking about his journal, three months of his writing irretrievably lost. "What do you mean play private detective?"

The photographer looked around warily.

"Sometimes," he said so softly that they had to lean forward to hear him, "sometimes it is possible, if one asks the right questions of the right people in the right barzulas, to find out something."

"What good is that?" asked the businessman. "If the police don't find them, I can't see how…."

"Mother of Jesus," the photographer exclaimed, "the police don't really care if they find your beloved possessions or not. They still get paid every week. But trust me, I know that for these thieves, it is easier sometimes to take a few hundred American dollars than to try and sell the stolen goods. You understand now?"

"Of course," said Christopher, a trickle of hope caught in his voice. "And if the stuff wasn't worth anything to them on the black market, it wouldn't cost too much to get it back, would it?"

"I don't know," said Harold stroking his beard. "If we're going to collect insurance, we must report it to the police."

"Bene," said the photographer, smiling now. "Report it, of course. But if you don't get satisfaction, come and see me tonight, after eight, at Barzula Sportivo on via Napoli. I will let you know if I've found out anything. I am lost without my camera anyway, so it is no problem at the same time to find out about your losses too. Ciao," he called as he left.

"What harm can it do if he makes enquiries?" Christopher said as they eyed the doorway through which the photographer had disappeared. The businessman shrugged his shoulders and slumped back into his chair to await the inspector.

Christopher wished that he had gone with the photographer. Having lived in Rome for the last eight months, he had become familiar with the unique bureaucracy that was Italy. He had learned that even a simple banking transaction took a dozen people several days to complete. The interminable siestas had almost driven him mad at first but now he was learning to live at the leisurely pace of the land.

A few minutes after four, a small, wiry man in uniform sauntered in, smiled and ducked into the office beyond the waiting room. The trio looked up and shuffled in their seats anticipating some action. Three-quarters of an hour later, the inspector reappeared, glanced quizzically at them, as if surprised that they were still there, and called Christopher into his office.

A few minutes later Christopher returned to the waiting room, a sheaf of papers and a pencil in his hands.

"Looks like that photographer was half right," he said.

Within half an hour all three were busy filling in the forms.

The businessman badgered the inspector, "Shouldn't you be assigning someone to get on the case immediately?"

The inspector rolled his eyes.

"Signor," he said, "we must have the information for our files and for the insurance, you know."

When all the papers were filled in and returned, the inspector spoke to them.

"Gentlemen," he said, "I will be honest with you. There is little hope of recovering your goods. Roma, as you know, is a very big city. The thieves are professionals, but the carabinieri will do everything in their power. Still, do not get your hopes high."

The three entered Barzula Sportivo promptly at eight. A few minutes later the photographer approached them, beaming. Slung around his neck was a Nikon with a massive telephoto lens.

"Do not look so sad friends," he said as he joined them

and ordered an Americano. "It is too wonderful to believe, is it not? I have my camera back."

"But how did you do it?" Christopher said. "The police said not even to hope."

The photographer sipped his drink. "Was I not right about our honourable carabinieri?" he said, poking the businessman lightly on the arm.

"You may have been right there," the businessman said, "and you may have your camera back but the thieves, no offence intended, are your countrymen. What good does it do us?"

"And they're certainly not going to repair the damage to my car or make up for the lost day of my vacation," said Harold.

"My friends, I regret you are right. The thieves are my compatriots and I am ashamed of what they have done to visitors to bella Roma. But I'm also your paesan. Did I not tell you? My father was a GI. He never married my mother but some days I feel so American. All three of you are like my brothers. Now come," he said, "let me buy you a drink in celebration of the return of my livelihood. Then you will see I have not let you down. I have not been so selfish just to get my camera back."

"My journal," Christopher said, "do you have it too?"

The photographer laughed. "It's not so simple, but I have made certain enquiries."

They sat silently as Gino, the photographer, spoke animatedly to several people at the bar. When he returned to the table he lowered his voice.

"I will tell you everything," he said and explained how through his connections and some American dollars, he had gotten back not only his camera but also information on their losses.

"You are fortunate my friends," he said. "I have learned that your stereo, your laptop, journal and briefcase have not yet been sold on the black market. I will be able to get these items back to you."

They could no longer doubt him. Gino knew exactly what they had lost and for the first time that long day, the three felt optimistic and confident as they signed over several American Express checks to him.

Gino was ecstatic as he took a picture of his new friends. If all went well, he promised to have their lost goods returned to them at breakfast the next day. He refused on his honour to take anything for his troubles.

"I only hope I can make your visit to the eternal city more memorable," he said before he swaggered out of the bar.

"Perhaps Gino's stuck in traffic," Christopher said to the others as they finished their third espresso in the bar the next day. But a gnawing doubt was growing in their hearts as they waited the morning away.

When the clock in the barzula struck noon, the businessman began to chuckle. Soon he was laughing loudly.

"Geez, what idiots we are," he said. "We've been duped twice by the same guy. I guess he and his cronies weren't satisfied with their first take and decided to have us pay him for the theft, too."

"I don't believe it," Christopher said, but he knew it was

true.

Still, he remained in the bar long after the other two had left, waiting for Gino and the return of his precious journal.

A Weekend Affair

After Paul took off with that Jezebel from his office, I was hard pressed to keep up the mortgage payments on the house. Since I needed very little space for my cat Natasha and my books, I decided to rent out the third floor. With its separate entrance and bathroom, it made for a cosy flat.

After running an ad on Craigslist for a month with no response, I'd almost given up hope of renting it. Then a man with a foreign accent called. He asked to see the flat that evening. Shortly before eight I positioned myself behind the drapes in the second floor bedroom. When the red Mercedes convertible parked in the driveway and a tanned man in his fifties emerged, I knew this was no ordinary tenant.

A shiver went through my body when I shook hands with Lucas Czerni.

"I'm looking for a quiet place. Private," he said as he wandered through the flat. "I don't have great needs. I only want it for weekends."

He fingered the mahogany chest of drawers in the bedroom.

"The antiques are charming," he said, "but I'll bring my own bed. A comfortable bed is so important."

"You live alone?" he asked as we entered my living room on the first floor to sign the lease.

I could feel his eyes appraising my sparse furnishings. He bent down to look through the books which were piled on every surface of the room.

"Flaubert, Tolstoy, Nabokov – even Balzac," he said and smiled. "Surely you have a European background."

I shook my head and felt myself blush.

"Not really, I just work in the library downtown and I like to read."

I offered him a drink but he was late for an engagement. He paid first and last month's rent in cash.

"Rent cheques will arrive in the mail the third week of every month," he said. "Please don't concern yourself about my comings and goings. I'm often abroad. I'll need an extra key if you have one. It's for a very close friend. I'm sure you understand."

I watched them move in that first weekend, Lucas and his friend. She was blonde, long-legged and voluptuous.

Jailbait, I muttered as I scrubbed the toilet bowl until it gleamed. Later I took a hot bath followed by a needle cold shower.

All that weekend and the next I thought that Lucas might drop by with a question about the flat or to borrow a book. But he didn't. In fact, I never spoke to him again.

Once or twice I went out when he drove up. He only smiled and waved as he sprinted up the stairs into his flat. I never did find out Lolita's name.

Every weekend they arrived separately. Once in the flat on Friday evening, they did not leave again until early Monday morning.

Having strangers in my house changed my routine too. I no longer went out at all on weekends and I must admit I became somewhat of a recluse.

Jennifer, a colleague from the library, wanted to drop by and I feigned illness. When Jim, a friend of Paul's, offered to clean the eaves, I told him rather bluntly that Lucas was going to do it. I told my mother that I had to work every weekend. I even cancelled the weekend papers and took the phone off the hook.

As landlady I wanted to be there in case Lucas needed something. I also pared down my activities to the bare essentials.

I found that if I stayed in my bedroom on the second floor and lay quite still, I could hear sounds and movements in the flat above. I even timed my visits to the bathroom with theirs.

Cocooning had its pluses. Lucas was a great and tireless lover. How many times, while gripping the sheets around my naked body and hugging a pillow between my moistened thighs, I tried not to call out as I listened breathlessly to Lolita's moans and murmurs of ecstasy.

It was only much later, exhausted and sweaty that I

would cry myself to sleep.

Then, as abruptly as they began, the lusty weekends ended. At first I thought the lovers must be on vacation, but soon the lost weekends added up to months. Yet the rent cheques continued to arrive, like my period, the third week of every month.

During those first missed weekends, I daren't go out, thinking Lucas might come. But later, I lost all expectation of his return and I returned to shopping, doing the laundry and vacuuming.

Yet not a weekend went by when I didn't think of him. Dozens of tawdry scenes played out in my head – accidental death, a fatal illness, a lovers' spat turned sour and permanent, missed communication, a forlorn spouse. If only Lucas had told me, had slipped a note in with the rent cheque. Instead I was left in limbo.

Winter turned into spring, spring into summer and still nothing except the damn rent cheques as regular as the seasons. If they had stopped I could search Lucas out, demand an explanation.

On a sweltering holiday weekend in August, I decided to check out the flat even though I knew I was breaking both the laws of privacy and the landlord/tenant act. I waited until after the witching hour on the off chance that Lucas would appear. Stealthy as a cat burglar and fortified with several glasses of wine, I crept up to the flat. My hands shook as I unlocked the door and turned on the light. It glowed red revealing a fetid shrine to Venus.

Heavy drapes shrouded all the windows. Erotic

paintings, sketches and photographs hung on walls that were covered in tapestries and brocades. Plump, tasseled velvet pillows were strewn on a red leather chaise lounge and plush sofas. Silken oriental rugs were flung helter-skelter over my grey broadloom. Desiccated flowers drooped in crystal vases. Candles, incense holders and wine glasses paid silent tribute to Bacchus. A musty smell hung like smoke over everything.

I must have fallen asleep on the unmade bed as at some point I became aware of mourning doves cooing outside the darkened window. Feeling unbearably hot and constricted, I tore my clothes off and staggered into the bathroom. Towels lay heaped on the floor; unguents and ointments lay ready to soothe bodies fresh from lovemaking.

I filled the tub with steamy water and passion fruit oil and lay there for what seemed like hours, gently caressing myself. Then dripping wet, I wandered naked through the rooms, my body vibrating with heat. I lay back on the bed and pressed pieces of his clothing to my body. Entwined in the silken sheets and rocking gently, I welcomed Lucas to my sanctuary.

My Life with Grandma

"Have a good day," she said as she dumped me at Rockcliffe Towers before eight on Sunday morning. I scowled but didn't say anything. We'd been having too many fights lately. I knew that no matter what I said I was stuck here for the day.

I unlocked the lobby doors and glanced back. Mom and her snazzy red MG were already gone. The lobby was deserted and I didn't have to wait for the elevator. In the elevator mirrors I could see myself seeing myself over and over again into infinity. This was way cool.

On grandma's floor, I hurried along the dim corridor past the crystal sconces which cast spooky shadows on the patterned walls. I had a key and grandma knew I was coming, but still I wished mom had come up with me.

When I opened the door, I was relieved to see grandma sitting near the window doing her needlepoint.

"Hello Matthew. Welcome. Where's your mother? Too

busy to even come up?"

"She said she'd pick me up around six and would see you then."

Grandma put down her canvas, heaved her bulk out of the chair and reached up to hug me. She brushed my cheeks with a dry kiss.

"Every time I see you, you seem to have shot up another foot. Have you had breakfast?"

Anticipating her home-made crepes with apricot jam, I lied, "No. Mom was late as usual so we rushed."

Grandma pursed her lips as she shuffled into the kitchen.

"I don't know about your mom. Always in a hurry. No time for anything. One day when it's too late, she'll realize what she's missed."

After breakfast grandma and I took the bus to Woodlands Cemetery on the outskirts of the city. She wanted to plant some geraniums on grandpa's grave.

"Your mother should have come with us," she said as we rode the bus. "Out of respect. It doesn't look good for her never to have visited when he was alive. Now, when he's dead, it's shameful. Your mother, always her own way."

I had only been to the cemetery once before when grandpa died. Dad still lived with us then and he came to the funeral, too. We all rode in a black limo. The driver jumped out to open and close the doors for us like we were rich. It was wicked.

Mom and grandma were dressed all in black and sat close together holding hands but didn't say a word during the entire trip from the funeral parlour to the church and then to the cemetery. Dad stared out the window.

I felt like I was in a dream, floating outside myself and just watching everything unfold. The cemetery was just like in *The Godfather*. The howling wind blew snow around us as we huddled close to the deep trench where they were going to put grandpa. Stacks of flowers in baskets and wreaths were heaped in a mound on the dirty snow next to the grave.

That was also the only time I'd been in a church. It was kind of creepy. Hundreds of candles flickered beside the altar which looked like a fancy stage. The place smelled bad and when the priest chanted, smoke rose all around the casket where grandpa lay. Grandma couldn't stop crying.

The windows and the sculptures along the sides of the church showed gruesome scenes of Jesus and other people being tortured. In one alcove blood seemed to drip from Jesus's wounds as he hung on the cross. Yucky gross.

Some friends of mine went to church every Sunday but we never went back. My mom said the pope and all the priests were corrupt and religion was just stories like fairy tales to keep people in line. She had been taught by nuns and priests so I guess she knew.

Grandma hadn't been to church since the funeral. She said she didn't believe much of anything anymore.

While grandma was planting the geraniums, I wandered amongst the tombstones, calculating the ages of the people who had died. I found three Matthews. One, Matthew Cassidy, had died at my age in 1926. I wondered what he had died from.

At the water tap, I filled a container and brought it to grandma.

"There, that's better," grandma said as she poured water over the plants. "Your grandpa never cared for flowers when he was alive but this shows that we haven't forgotten him."

She looked over the neighbouring gravestones.

"Such neglect. When I was young we would come here every Sunday. People didn't forget then. Nowadays everyone is too damn busy."

Grandma began to cry and I didn't know what to do.

"Is anybody else you know buried here?" I said.

She dabbed at her eyes.

"Come. I'll show you where some of your relatives are."

She hobbled along the manicured pathways, twisting and turning precisely before stopping at one grave after another. I saw the modest grey granite monuments of my great-grandparents on my mother's side, a spinster grand-aunt who lived to 92, and a cousin who had died in childbirth.

We visited the area where what grandma called "the innocents" were buried. Row upon row of small white blocks marked the resting place of infants who had died before being baptised. One block was etched with grandma's last name. It belonged to her only son – my mother's elder brother. He was born dead and didn't even have a first name.

My stomach was growling and I was dying of thirst by the time we reached Uncle Jimmie's grave. I stifled a yawn as grandma told me again about Jimmie who was electrocuted while repairing hydro wires. He was only 23.

"The ladder was sitting in water and Jimmie wasn't

wearing his safety boots. He was out drinking the night before with your grandpa. He must have been too tired to remember to put the boots on."

I had heard the story a thousand times before but that didn't stop her.

"Now that was a day I'll never forget with all the reporters coming to the house. Jimmie's accident, it made the front page of *The Spectator*. Jimmie's mother, your great-grandmother was wailing. And your grandpa — that changed him forever. He'd always been a drinker but after his brother's death, he drank more and more. I think he blamed himself for letting his kid brother get drunk on a week night."

Grandma was wiping tears from her eyes when I heard something. I turned and was flattened by a huge dog. His owner yanked on its leash and got him off me. My t-shirt was torn and I could see claw marks on my chest.

The man held the mastiff as his companion rushed over.

"Are you okay honey? What a shame Dante's torn your shirt."

"Sorry," the man said as he edged closer while trying to hold back the dog. "I'm sure you'll be okay. You can see it's just a scratch. I don't know what got into Dante. He must have thought you were playing. Moved suddenly, didn't you?"

Then the woman handed me a twenty dollar bill.

"Here, you can buy a new t-shirt," she said and before we could say anything they hurried away.

"Jesus Christ," grandma said. "Your mother will kill me."

Then she looked at my torn shirt. Huge bruises in the shape of the dog's paws were forming on my chest.

"We can try to hold your t-shirt together with these," she said and took a string of safety pins from her purse. "That way no one will notice on the way home."

It was then that I began to cry.

"Grandma, what if the dog was rabid. Shouldn't I go to the hospital and get shots?"

"Don't worry. They were polite," she said. "The dog looked healthy and clean. They were a nice couple – well dressed. They gave you money without us even asking. But I don't know what we're going to tell your mother."

She needn't have worried. Mom got to grandma's late and spent about half an hour talking about her latest boyfriend problems. When grandma finally got a word in and told her about the attack, mom turned around and looked at me sprawled in front of the TV.

"Matthew come here and show your mother your chest," grandma said.

As I walked towards her, mom began to laugh.

"Jesus mother," she said to grandma, "at least your safety pins came in handy. It's quite the rip. I can see why they gave him twenty dollars for a new shirt."

It was shortly after that that I came to live with grandma. Mom said it would only be for a few months – that she needed time to get herself together.

"It'll be good for grandma too. She's never gotten over grandpa's death. Just imagine living alone after spending nearly sixty years with someone," she said.

During the week it wasn't bad. I went to school. Grandma cooked supper. Then I watched TV, played Nintendo, did my homework, had a shower, and went to bed.

On weekends though it got weird. Grandma would open a bottle of sherry and pull out the photo albums. She wanted me to write down the dates and who the people in the pictures were.

"Your mother's not interested, so Matthew, it's up to you to remember."

I had hoped we'd run out of photo albums but each Friday night grandma drank her sherry and pulled another album from the mahogany buffet. She sipped and talked. After about an hour she'd be quiet for a long time. That's when I'd turn on the TV.

Later, when I went to bed, grandma would be snoring, her head resting on a photo album on the kitchen table.

One day I counted the photo albums — there were seventeen. Flipping through them, I noticed that each one ended with pictures of gravestones. The last page of one of the albums had grandpa's gravestone in the snow and then with flowers planted around it. The spooky thing was the stone also had grandma's name and birth date carved on it. After that there were no more pictures, just blank pages.

For Family Studies we were supposed to do a project on our home environment. I took a few snapshots of grandma when she was busy around the apartment watering plants, cooking or watching TV. I asked her to pose so I could take portraits, too.

"You don't want pictures of me. I'm too old."

"How else can I do my report? You're all I've got for a home environment, grandma. You don't want me to fail, do you?"

She stared at me. Then she sighed and sat very still while I shot. I also shot close-ups of her hands doing needlepoint and playing solitaire. I wrote an essay called *My Life with Grandma* and then arranged the photos around it on Bristol board.

I thought the project was okay, although the essay part was kind of boring. I added the story of the dog attack at the cemetery to liven it up a bit. As for the pictures, most of the snapshots were slightly out of focus. In each portrait, grandma with her blank eyes staring, looked kind of frozen, like she belonged in a wax museum – or an old photo album. But I thought the close-ups were pretty good. I hadn't noticed until I saw the prints that her hands were like my mother's, smooth and delicate.

Before taking it to school, I showed the project to grandma. She read the essay and looked at the pictures for a long time. Then she began to cry.

"It's no good Matthew. This is wrong. Lydia must come and get you. I'll call her today."

Only the Lonely

It jumped out at her. Afternoons free? Family man bored with present situation seeks stimulating, attractive woman to be his mistress. Reply Box 1696.

A tiny item just five lines high in the personal column of the Star. She read it again aloud, pausing after the word *mistress.*

This was 21st century Toronto, not Paris in the 1890s. Surely people didn't have mistresses today. Here.

Mistress. The word sounded marvelous. There was no denying the fact. Mistress. A kept woman. Kept for love.

She tore her eyes and mind away and scanned the next item. A former police detective will conduct your investigations. Discreet, professional. Box 1347. And the next. Anxious, suicidal, in crisis? Call Distress Centre. 416-347-8737. But her head refused to co-operate. Her eyes swung back. Afternoons free? The answer, of course, was yes. Yes. But could she? Dare she?

Mistress. She whispered the seductive word as she shuffled in her terry bathrobe into the kitchen. I'm his mistress. She phrased it silently first and then whispered the word as she plugged in the kettle. Her dark eyes glazed over last night's spaghetti-stained plates.

The phone rang. Her eyes refocused. She smoothed her hair. Could it be him? Ridiculous. She hadn't even written the letter yet. Frowning, she picked up the phone.

A familiar voice chattering. Her mother. Her cheery tone made her gag. David, her, the kids. Yes, all were fine. The arthritis was bad today. Must be the weather. Quiet here now that Jason is in school. Must visit soon.

The kettle whistled shrilly. She poured the bubbling water into her coffee mug. Thought of David, Jennifer and Jason. Her family. She was mistress. Mistress of the house. There was a world of difference between the two.

How long had it been since she had written a letter? Dear Sir. Dear Mr. Family Man. Dear Lover. Lover – simple, tantalizing, sweet.

Lover, I'll meet you at the Park Plaza. Thursday at two. Wear a pink carnation. I'll do the same. With anticipation, your mistress.

Her first love letter, painstakingly rewritten until every word was just right. Then slowly copied in a graceful script with a fine-nibbed fountain pen onto cream-coloured stationery. Sprayed with eau de cologne and sealed with a kiss.

Down the lane to the mail box. Stood there, loathe to let it go. Scared. But she knew she must now, or always wonder.

Mail picked up at eleven. Next day delivery guaranteed. Thursday afternoon then. At two.

A whirlwind of activity in preparation for meeting her lover. Would she bring him home so soon? No matter. All was ready. The house never looked better and neither did she, mistress of the house.

Pins and needles. Needles and pins. Alive, alive-o!

Noon. Two more hours to go. She closed her eyes and tried to imagine him. Family man. Opened them with a start. All she could picture was David, her husband. Lover drew a blank.

Clock-watcher. Walked for the tenth time in as many minutes into the bedroom. The master bedroom. Clean white sheets on the queen-sized bed.

Stood brazenly in front of the full-length mirror in her never before worn black lace bra and panties. Eyed herself critically. Wondering if he would find her attractive? Stimulating?

36 years old. She felt like a 16-year-old waiting for her first date.

Suddenly she sat down and put her head in her hands. A moan escaped her and then another. She felt doomed. Sixteen years of marriage and it had come to this. Unfaithfulness. Infidelity. Adultery.

She twisted her gold wedding band, glanced at it and knew. Knew she still had time. Time to change her mind. She need not go. The letter was anonymous. No one would know. Not now or ever. Only her. It would be her secret.

But what about regrets? The regrets that would come

swiftly and brutally to torment her until … until the day she died. Death by regret and frustration.

One o'clock. She got up, her jaw set in a do or die, now or never attitude. She straightened her pantyhose and felt her thighs, still firm after 16 years of marriage and two children. Slipped into her soft knit, special occasion dress. Smiled at her reflection and remembered the last time she wore it. Mother's Day.

She picked up the framed pictures from her dresser. Her kids. Bright and beautiful — everything a mother could want. But they were growing up, and away. She knew only too well what a clinging mother was like and she had no intention of repeating her own mother's folly. But now that Jason was in school, she was lonely. Bitterly lonely and alone.

As she carefully replaced the pictures, she caught a glimpse of her face in the mirror. She reached up and touched it. Could that be her? That tired worn face marked with despair.

She forced herself to smile, but she had already recognized it. It was her mother's face. And it was hers.

She hurried now or she would be late. Tried to shake the fear that lay deep within. Hummed a tune. Thought gaily of the adventure that was to come. Sprayed expensive cologne lavishly and on parts of her body she'd never have dared to before.

A last glance, a toss of her hair, and she was leaving her house behind her.

She remembered when she was almost there. The pink carnation. It had been her idea. Corny perhaps, but how else would they recognize each other. He wouldn't have Box 1696 tattooed on his forehead. And she, she no longer had faith in destiny nor belief in love at first sight.

She bought one for fifty cents in a little flower shop that smelled funereal. Cloying. She could hardly wait to get out into the fresh air. But once outside she stopped and raised the flower to her nose. Should she wear it or hide it in her purse until she saw just who this family man was?

Slowly she walked past the fashionable shop windows, debating this dilemma. Stopped at a crosswalk and when the light turned green, she put the flower carefully into her purse. With a surge of confidence she realized that the power to decide the outcome of the affair still lay with her.

Seated in the candlelit dining room of the Park Plaza, she glanced around. Her eyes strained through the dim light trying to make out the people at other tables. Trying to find the one lone man who would be sporting a pink carnation. The one man who would change her life.

Abruptly, a thought crossed her mind, almost smothering her. What if he had put the carnation in his pocket, just as she had in her purse? A deadlock. Two losers.

She glanced at her watch, seven past two, and looked up toward the doorway. A tall and handsome man stood alone, surveying the dining room. She smiled to herself, knew instantly that it was him, and knew too that he would surpass her wildest fantasies. In a flash she opened her purse and her fingers clasped the bloom. All the while her eyes never left that glorious, soon-to-be-hers man. Lover.

A moment later her face crumpled. Next to him,

appearing suddenly, as if by some cruel twist of fate, stood a woman. The man smiled, embraced her, and together they made their way to a dark and intimate corner table. Two lovers.

Ashamed of her impulsiveness, she snapped her purse shut and ordered a double martini. She sat still for what seemed like ages – waiting. Expectantly waiting.

She had to pee but knew that if she left, he would come. Knew it as well as she knew anything. It was just the way it would be. Had to be.

Suddenly, another man stood at the doorway, calmly surveying the room. She gasped. Him! In a panic, she wondered what she could say when he saw her. How could she explain her presence, here, now?

She was stunned, afraid, confused. How could he be here, now? Then a sudden thought flitted through her head. She glanced at his familiar jacket, saw the pink carnation and started to laugh. Laughed in pain so great, the tears rolled down her cheeks.

So this then was Box 1696, the bored family man, her David.

Hesitating only a moment, she took her pink carnation from her purse and pinned it on her dress. She would meet her lover, and he, his mistress.

Fragments

I

One could expect much lamentation had my father's family been larger, but we were few. My mother had died twenty years earlier and I was an only child. His sister and her child lived in Germany but my father had not seen them since he emigrated to Canada in 1950.

So what was I to make of the outpourings of grief from the dozen strangers who turned up on that cold February day to pay their respects? I'd always known my father as a loner, a friendless man who treasured his solitude, his music, and his books. That day I learned for the first time that he had sung in a barber shop quartet, loved euchre, and was quite the charmer on the dance floor.

"Your father had such a zest for living," said Greg who had worked side by side with him thirty years earlier as a welder. "Nothing ever got him down."

"Always popular with the women," said Victor, another

of his white-haired cronies, "but I could never figure out why. Sure, he was handsome, but there was something more that women adored. See Pat and Jean over there. That's why they're here crying their eyes out."

I glanced at the two elderly ladies weeping together in a corner. The tall, slim one kept tying and untying the Hermes scarf draped over her cashmere sweater while the more grandmotherly woman patted her eyes with a lace hankie. I could see that both must have been quite striking years ago.

"A true gentleman," Jean said later as I helped her with her Persian lamb coat. "We'll miss him a lot. I don't think you knew him the way we did dear. Still, it must be hard. Such a loss."

Pat wept as she grasped my hands.

"I'm sorry, but we were so close these last few years."

My father's death wasn't a great loss to me. It was more an inconvenience. He had for ten years lived alone in a seniors' apartment building. We rarely spoke. I had never met his friends and was surprised by their warm recollections.

II

The mystery of my father's life was heightened when I came into possession of three odd items that he left me in his will. As sole beneficiary I would have received these items anyway. Yet my father had specified that I was to get a beer stein, a walking stick, and an old cavalry sabre.

The beer stein was one I had seen sitting on a shelf in my parents' house but had never paid much attention to. I don't think it was ever used. A typical Bavarian one litre stein, it was made of heavy grey stoneware decorated with a rich blue art nouveau motif. A hinged pewter lid had the word *Heimat* etched into it in old German script.

My father had used the walking stick as a cane up until the day he died. Well worn, it was covered with metal badges commemorating various parks in Germany. As a child when I had asked him about the colourful emblems, he eagerly told me that he had hiked in those parks as a young man before the Second World War. With great enthusiasm he urged me to start hiking the Bruce Trail which was close to our home. He said that vigorous walking in the outdoors would make me strong and fit. His incessant lectures on the joys of hiking were the only memories of his life in Germany that I remember him sharing.

The third item was something I had never seen before, a magnificent steel sabre carved with cavalry designs. It bore the name: Kronenberg Regiment. The sabre's lower end and tip were much dented and nicked.

Was it his? From the war that he never talked about? Had he actually used the sabre? I regretted now that I had never asked him about his wartime experiences.

These artifacts, along with the cardboard box containing his ashes, lay on the coffee table in the living room for a few days. Then, expecting company, I put them far back on the shelf in the front hall closet amongst a jumble of hats, scarves and gloves, and forgot about them.

III

Months later, while getting stuff ready for a lawn sale, I

found the box again. I picked it up. It crumbled at my touch, scattering ashes and tiny bone fragments all over the coats and jackets in the closet.

"Damn it all," I said to my wife who was carting a box of old dishes to the front porch. "Goddamn mice must have gnawed right through this."

I held several pieces of shredded cardboard in my hands. I had meant to get an urn, or scatter the ashes on the lake at the cottage, but had not gotten around to it yet.

"Should I get the vacuum?" my wife said as I was seized by a violent sneezing fit.

"Jesus, Sharon," I said between sneezes, "this is my father, all that's left of him."

I spent the next half hour meticulously shaking ashes off the clothing and gathering up the particles into a plastic margarine container.

"Goddamn mice. We'd better get a cat," I said as I joined my wife who was overseeing the lawn sale from the porch.

She looked at me but said nothing.

An old man sweating in the heat of the day held up the beer stein.

"How much?" he asked with a thick German accent like my father's.

"Ten dollars. It's an antique from Germany. My father brought it here after the war."

"An antique?"

Clutching the stein in his gnarled hands, he hobbled toward me and smiled.

"It is from Munich. I had one just like it. Shattered when they bombed the whole block where I lived. Nothing left but rubble and ashes."

"You actually drank out of it?" I said hoping to keep him interested in the purchase.

Holding onto the stein, the man sat down heavily on one of the director's chairs that we were selling. He wiped his brow with an already damp, cotton handkerchief.

"Of course," he said breathing heavily, "many litres, night after night in the *bierhalle*. We were young then; we sang *ein prosit, gemutlichkeit* many times. Yes, those were the good times, before the war changed us, changed everything. The beer never tasted as good in Canada. Never."

He ran his thick fingers tenderly over the stein's raised design. Then looked at me piercingly.

"Let me try out this stein before I pay you. Ten dollars is a lot of money — even for memories."

"Clever bugger," I said to my wife as I went to get a beer from the fridge. "I should up the price to include the beer."

The can of Coors didn't even half fill the stein. The old man closed his pale blue eyes as he gulped the cold brew.

"Yes," he said. "I remember. We were always laughing. The noise, lots of smoke, music, bright lights, and always friends singing together. We were happy. We were in love, and full of dreams."

He paused and drank again.

"All gone then. All gone now. *Heimat*, my homeland."

He sat with his eyes closed clutching the beer stein for so long that I began to worry whether the cold beer, the heat and his age would do him in, right in the middle of my lawn sale.

Eventually he roused himself, struggled up and looked around at the tables heaped with household items, trinkets and books. He shook his head.

"Selling your father's past are you? For shame, for shame."

He thrust the beer stein into my hands.

"Rinse this for me now."

When I returned with the stein, he was fingering some of my father's old tools. I wanted him to leave.

"You can have those if you want." My hands shook as I handed him the wet stein. "I've no use for them."

He picked up the tools and laid them reverently in his canvas shopping bag. He nudged a ten dollar bill from his wallet and pressed it into my hand.

"Your father, I think, was a good man," he said.

"A good German," he called back as he shambled down the street.

IV

A few days later my doctor told me I should exercise more. He recommended walking as a non-strenuous activity that I might enjoy. I thought of my father's old walking stick and took it from the hall closet. It still had particles of ash and dust on it.

I planned to hike in a nearby ravine for only an hour or so, but as I walked, my mind wandered to my father. Lost in thought, I found myself in a barren part of the woods that contained seven large boulders in a circle. I sat on the ground to rest my back against a boulder and fell asleep.

I dreamt that I was hiking in a forest. I was wearing stiff leather shorts and carrying my walking stick. My long, strong limbs climbed nimbly over the uneven trail. I felt the warm wind caress my face as the sun beat warmly on my hair and back. The smell of wild mushrooms, moss and ferns overwhelmed. I heard a laugh echo cleanly through the forest. I turned and smiled at the athletic-looking girl with short blonde hair striding toward me.

She laughed again as she stripped off her clothes. I found myself wrapped in her arms in the midst of a cool stream. Moaning with pleasure she kept calling me Karl – my father's name. Then a noise, like a shot, rang out and I rose to see where it had come from. When I turned back, Magdalen, for that was her name, was gone. I thrashed frantically about in the water, calling her name over and over again. Then I woke up.

That night and the night after, I had the dream again. The rerun always ended suddenly, like a sprocket hole tearing on a piece of film. My lost Magdalen.

I was shaking when I awoke and reached out to clutch my sleeping wife.

V

A few months later my aunt in Germany died. I had never met her; she and my father had not been close. Along with the notice of her death, my cousin sent me pictures of my father from her mother's photo album.

I gasped when I saw the first few. A lean, tall man with a broad grin, wearing traditional *lederhosen*, was hiking in the woods. He carried my father's walking stick. The inscription on the back of the photos was *Karl, Schwartzwald, 1935.* Another photo showed my father, young and dashing in a military uniform, proudly holding the sabre that he had handed down to me.

My hands trembled as I hurried through the photos until I found what I was looking for – the girl in my dreams. She stood jauntily atop a huge boulder, mugging for the photographer. I turned the photo over and read *Magdalen, Schwartzwald, 1935.*

The other photos showed my father and my mother, Hilda, after the war on their wedding day, on their honeymoon in Strasbourg, and boarding the *Empress of Norway* which took them to their new life in Canada.

I stared at the photos for a long time. Then I went to the closet. I found the sabre. I took it out of its scabbard and examined it closely. As I slid my fingers over it, I cut myself and watched, mesmerized, as drops of blood mingled with ash particles and oozed into the grooves of the well-worn blade.

VI

The next day I bought a ticket to visit my father's homeland. I took the walking stick and my father's ashes with me. After visiting my cousin, my only remaining blood relative, I went for a hike in the Black Forest. I scattered the last physical remains of my father at the end of a steep hiking path along a clear, fast stream. I watched the swirling water carry the ashes and bone fragments deeper into the forest of his youth. I waited until the last of them melded into the water and disappeared.

I was a good son; I had brought my father home.

When I Heard the Gypsy Music

The year was 1956 and a world away in my father's birthplace, revolution blossomed briefly before six thousand tanks and tens of thousands of Soviet troops crushed the hope of a nation. Two hundred thousand Hungarians fled their homeland. Among them was my eight-year-old second cousin, Agnes, and her parents.

Their arrival, in their church-going clothes with no possessions, at my grandmother's house on a Sunday morning dramatically changed my world, too.

The story of their risky flight from communism was told to my grandparents in Hungarian, a language that I could not understand. For although my father was born in Hungary, my mother, whom he met in Canada, was an Italian immigrant. They spoke English to each other and swore that their Canadian born children would speak only the language of their new land.

Agnes became the focus of my life when I decided to

teach her to speak English. We sat in my grandmother's bedroom and I would point at something and name it. Agnes would repeat the word several times. She learned quickly and we progressed, object by object, room by room.

The refugees settled in a rooming house nearby and it was decided that Agnes would be going to my school. I was delegated to bring her to school, look after her there, and bring her home again.

Until then, going to school had been sheer hell for me. Everything from my funny-sounding last name to my homemade clothes ensured that I didn't fit in.

How I had prayed for an end to roll call and how I envied kids with simple Anglo names. I tried on substitute names as though they were dresses. I knew that if I could miraculously have one of those names my entire life would change.

My mother was thrifty and talented with a needle so I became the only child in my poor Catholic school to wear clothes in the style of Princess Anne — smocked and lacy with puffed sleeves, ribbons, and bows. My grandfather, a shoemaker, made me shiny black patent leather shoes and red leather sandals. But to me, homemade meant poor. More than anything, I wanted store-bought clothes and shoes like my classmates.

Exiled to the back of the classroom because of my height further fuelled my feeling of not belonging. Like many tall children, my arms and legs often seemed detached not only from my body but also from my brain. And contrary to popular belief about tall people, I was lousy at sports, especially basketball. I still carry the shame of being last chosen for any team.

But with the sudden and awesome responsibility of taking Agnes to school, my embarrassed awkwardness disappeared.

Sister Carmela and my classmates were as fascinated with this exotic creature who had parachuted into our classroom as I was. Although she looked like us, Agnes was part of something bigger Sister Carmela said. She was an escapee from communism and a symbol of the western world's fight against the Red Menace.

For me, Agnes gave substance to the Hungarian half of my heritage. Her last name was also strange sounding and hard to pronounce, but the events surrounding her were reported in the daily newspaper and on radio. Now everyone seemed to know about Hungary and Hungarians. Soon they would all be eating cabbage rolls and paprikash.

Although I knew no more Hungarian than my classmates, as her cousin, I was appointed Agnes's interpreter and general keeper. At recess, classmates who had previously ignored me, clustered around to marvel at Agnes. They touched her long golden hair and tried to get her to pronounce their names and play with them.

Agnes blossomed with all the attention and I, as her mentor, cousin, and self-appointed best friend, basked in it as well. Because of Agnes, I was no longer the last chosen for a team in phys ed class. Everyone wanted to show their generosity by picking her first and as her interpreter I came with her – a package deal.

Agnes was shorter than me so she could wear the clothes I'd grown out of. Seeing her wearing my smocked dresses of the previous year transformed them from homemade into something magical.

"Pretty dress. Agnes looks so nice," my classmates would coo in exaggeratedly simple English as I stood like a proud mother hen on the sidelines.

Unfortunately, my favoured role all too soon came to an end when Agnes's parents found jobs, rented an apartment in the west end of the city and transferred Agnes to another school.

Nearly a year went by before I saw her again. Although we lived only a few miles away, we may as well have been an ocean apart. My mother felt uncomfortable around the foreigners who continued to speak Hungarian in her presence. And my father felt the new immigrants were undermining him with his parents. On several occasions they had complained to my grandmother about his drinking and gambling.

I think the falling out with my new found relatives had a lot to do with my father. He was more like hot-tempered Ricky on the *I Love Lucy* show and loud-mouthed Ralph Kramden of *The Honeymooners* than the polite dads depicted in *Leave It to Beaver* and *Father Knows Best.*

So it came as quite a surprise when my mother told me I had been invited to Agnes's ninth birthday party. I spent a week choosing a book as a birthday present. It had to be simple enough so that Agnes could understand it and also a book that I treasured. I decided on *The Diary of Anne Frank* and took special care to wrap it and enclose a card to my special and still best friend. My mother suggested I take some of my old clothes to Agnes as well.

The party included children from Agnes's new school and many recent refugees, both children and adults. The air was filled with the warm smell of Hungarian home cooking mixed with acrid cigarette smoke. A cacophony of people talked loudly in several languages while children squabbled and a fiddler played raucous gypsy music.

As the birthday girl, Agnes was the centre of attention. When I finally got to speak with her, I was amazed at how articulate and charming she had become. She had hardly a trace of an accent yet switched effortlessly into rapid Hungarian when talking to her parents or other adults. She introduced me to the other children as her cousin and first Canadian friend. A perfect hostess, Agnes made sure I was given enough to eat and drink. I marveled at how gracefully grown up she had become in the year since I'd last seen her.

After awhile, Agnes's mother brought out a huge multi-layered cake with hardened candy on top and nine sparkling candles. The fiddler played *Happy Birthday*. Agnes made her wish and blew out the candles.

Then it was time to open the presents. There were lots of them — money and gold jewellery, several dolls, paper cut-outs, records and a miniature metal kitchen complete with tiny pots and pans, dishes and spoons. When she opened my gift, Agnes smiled charmingly and thanked me profusely. But I could tell something was wrong.

"Have you already read Anne Frank's diary?" I asked.

"No I haven't, but I've heard of it. It's about that Jewish girl who they say was killed by the Nazis. It doesn't really interest me," she said and tossed it on the table with the other gifts.

Next, she opened the bag with my old dresses in it.

"Oh," she said, "I've grown as big as you now so I don't think these will fit."

Seeing that I was near to tears, she added, "Don't worry, my mother will send them to the old country. I'm sure someone there will get some use from them."

Her friends came over and she moved away, drifting into the swirling smoke, the spicy odours, and the squawky gypsy music.

Soon after, I left the party and, fearful of taking the wrong bus, I walked all the way home through the cold, grey evening counting television aerials along the way.

Bright Lines

I made it a rule never to drink alone, but here I am again by myself at four in the afternoon gleefully uncorking a bottle of oak-aged Chardonnay.

Today I'm celebrating life. Being alive. Being able to sit in my sun-dappled kitchen and enjoy a glass of chilled white wine. Nothing wrong with that, is there?

Well, maybe there is a problem. I've managed nine months without the sacred fruit of the vine and I'm about to ruin it all for a glass full of pleasure.

That's life, isn't it? You start something with the best of intentions and then it ends. Everything comes to an end.

Why today? Why now? There's nothing special about today. That's the whole point, don't you see? If it were a special occasion or if I'd encountered something distressing, then I would be drinking for a reason. The whole point is I can drink, just like anyone, to celebrate the day. Any day. Today!

I think I should tweet my friends this profound insight, but I don't really want them to know that I haven't been drinking for the past nine months and that now I'm going to break the spell and have a glass.

It's kind of sad though, isn't it? Nine months. Why not head for an even ten, or a year, and then break my self-imposed sobriety?

But on the plus side, I'm going to drink mindfully. I'm going to take my time and not just guzzle it down. Savour it. Treat it as a sacrament – a blessing from our fertile mother earth.

Fruit of the vine, how divine! Already the poetry flows from my lips.

And I will have just one glass, for sure. I don't think my clean liver could take the jolt from too much vino after doing without for so long. The label says 13% alcohol. A bit high perhaps. I'll Google the time it takes for my liver to detoxify the 13% and then I'm good to go.

Big mistake. I roamed about the web a bit and discovered tons of depressing news. Cold weather killed two million fish on Chesapeake Bay. Arkansas rained blackbirds when 10,000 fell dead from the sky. Forty thousand velvet swimming crabs, along with starfish, lobsters, sponges, sea anemones – all dead of hypothermia. Hundreds of snapper fish in New Zealand starved to death due to weather. Fifty jackdaw birds in Stockholm and 450 birds in Louisiana – all dead. Now I really need a drink.

It's like the proverbial canary in the coal mine warning us. But is anyone listening? And even if we hear, what can we do except worry and maybe have a drink?

I did find out that one glass of wine will pass through the liver of an average-sized person in one hour. Not so bad then, is it?

I couldn't find its effect on brain cells though. But there's loads of information about the health effects of wine, especially red wine with all its antioxidants and other good things that benefit the heart and delay aging.

I read about a woman who lived to be 104 and indulged in a shot of whiskey every day before bed. You go, girl!

I can already taste the wine's cool tartness, feel the tingly burst of pleasure buds on my tongue, smell the sweet aroma of sun-infused grapes. All this and it's healthy too.

Shouldn't drink though without a bite to eat. I'll get a few tidbits together first, even though I know I always eat too much when I drink. And then I need more to drink. So it goes – the circular nature of life.

Why had I stopped? I remember writing down all the reasons to stop or to continue drinking. Mostly, I worried about alcohol's effect on my liver and on my brain cells.

But I'm an independent, healthy grown-up. I should be able to treat myself now and then. Besides, no one need know, and even if they did, they probably wouldn't care. More likely they'd be pleased in a *welcome back* kind of way. My not drinking seemed to make some people a touch uncomfortable when they were indulging. Not enough to give up the forbidden fruit themselves but enough to add a *frisson* of guilt to their sinful pleasure.

Stopping and thinking about your actions even just for a

moment, that's what's it all about, isn't it?

Drinking is so automatic pilot: "Yes, thanks a glass of Sauvignon blanc please. How delightful. It's good to get together. We should do this more often. Just a bit more. Have to work this afternoon. If I drink too much I'll just want to sleep. Oh yes, I'll have dessert. Why not? Diet's already ruined and I want to celebrate."

Am I going to regret this tomorrow? Well nine months is a really long time – the longest I've ever gone without, except for when I was pregnant. And briefly, when the kids were little and I worried about the effect on them of seeing their mommy always with a wine glass in her hand. What kind of a role model would I be? But then, of course, what kind of a role model is a depressed and uptight parent?

After the accident I was on meds and couldn't drink. And after six months without, well, it was easy to just continue. I'm proud of myself. Pleased as punch! I went through recovery, rehab, travelling, funerals, and weddings – all without a drink.

When people asked I just shook my head and said, "I'm on medication, not supposed to drink". That was so easy.

It's always been easier to not drink at all, rather than drink moderately. Hate that word, don't you? Moderately – it's so run of the mill, middle of the road. And what does it mean anyway? I've always prided myself on being an all or nothing kind of person. Intense. Yes!

To be sure, when I didn't have alcohol in my system, my brain fog occasionally lifted. I could identify things I wanted to do, make some plans, dream a little. But now I'm really not sure I want to do much of anything.

When I used to drink, parts of the day disappeared and I could seldom remember where the time went. Not drinking gave me more time. Funny how 24 hours could seem so long then. I could fill it with all sorts of good and healthy things. I could read without falling asleep, too. And I read a lot. I had to keep my mind occupied or it would wander into the abyss. That was scary.

But I don't mind if part of today disappears. I've decided to treat myself. The goodies are out on a plate. Now I'll rinse a glass and get the corkscrew. Hope it still works, not like the time I was stuck in a hotel room about to have a glass and my dollar-store corkscrew wouldn't turn – just gouged the cork. What a mess! I had to let the wine drip into my glass from the pin-sized opening. Still it tasted good even with the cork bits mixed in.

Note to self – buy only screw-top bottles of wine.

People may think that my accident was caused by alcohol and that's why I no longer drink. It wasn't though. In fact, I had stopped drinking a month before the accident after a particularly uninhibited party.

The day after that party, I decided to change my life. Most of all I wanted to end the non-stop obsessive-compulsive thinking, thinking, thinking. The mind-dance around *will I?* or *won't I?* have a drink pre-dinner, with dinner, post-dinner, at the theatre, at lunch, with friends, with relatives, after a flap at work, after grocery shopping, after reading the newspaper, after anything. Everything seemed to cry out for a drink. A drink so I could carry on.

But sometimes, like now, I just want to chill out, relax, let go and be happy like the carefree people in TV commercials and magazine ads. They're enjoying life in a laidback kind of way and not just in exotic locations but in ordinary places as well. Yessiree, drinking is our #1 stress-buster!

And how else can I turn off my thoughts? I read somewhere that Eric Clapton said drinking filled all his thoughts until he prayed for help. I'm not sure about the praying or needing help, but I can identify with his mindset. We don't hear much about Eric anymore. Celebrity suicides, car accidents and divorces make headlines, while recovery rarely makes the news.

Even though I'm not an alcoholic, I admit that I seek out stories about famous alcoholics both dead and those still alive, and I understand their struggles. In spite of their wealth and success they are just like me, fighting their own demons.

But I am careful. I've made many rules to drink by: only one glass with dinner; only drink when socializing; never drink alone; only wine, not the hard stuff; sip slowly; only on weekends, never during the week.

These clear, simple, unambiguous rules are my bright lines. But you know, bright lines are made to be broken. Just a little bit. Sometimes. Cheers.

About the Author

Linda Joyce Ott is a writer and artist. *Open Wounds, Secret Obsessions* is her first book of fiction.

Linda honed her creative writing over the course of a successful career as a writer, editor and communications consultant. She lives in Hamilton, Ontario, Canada with her husband, Günter, and two cats, Scampi and Squeak.

To see her art and photography, visit her website at http://www.lindajoyceott.com or her blog at http://www.optimismofcolor.com